JACK FINCH BELIEVES IN GHOSTS

connor bryan

Sun Cat
Publishing

First paperback edition October 2022

Book design by Connor Bryan

ISBN 979-8-9864849-0-7 (trade paperback)
ISBN 979-8-9864849-2-1 (e-book)

Published by Sun Cat Publishing

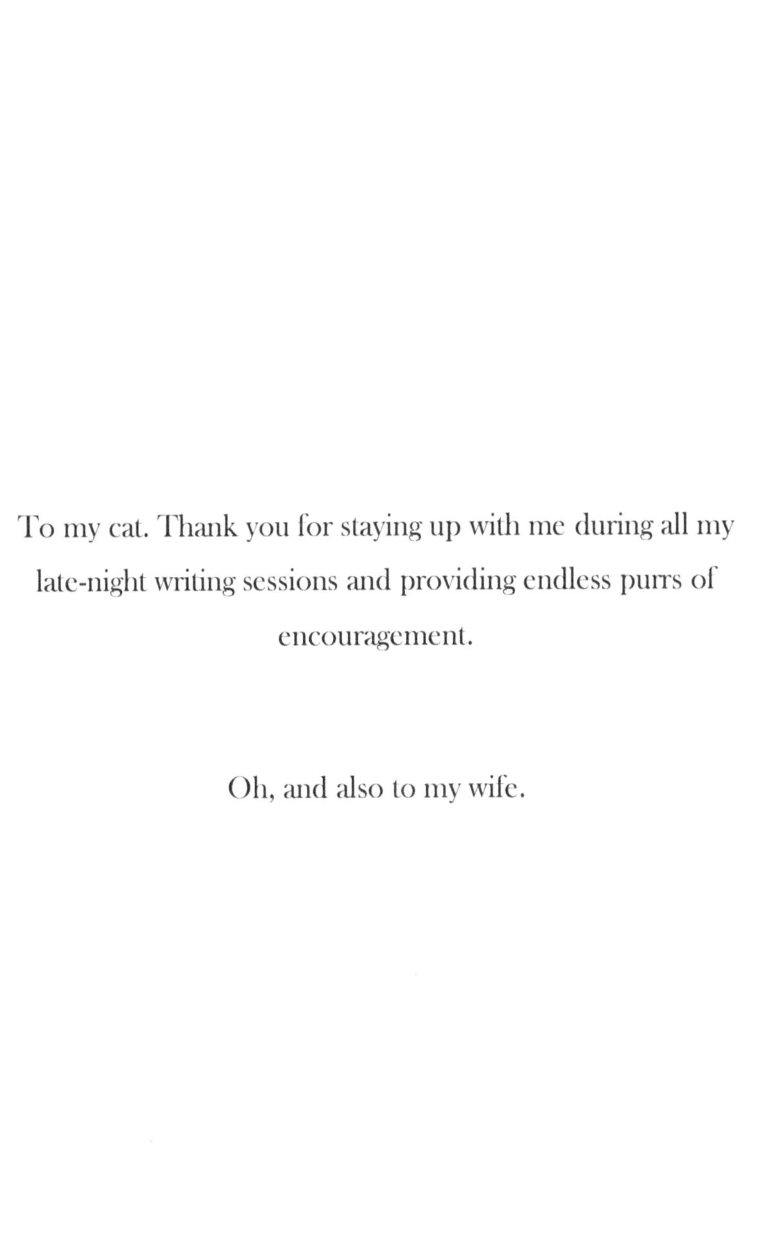

To my cat. Thank you for staying up with me during all my late-night writing sessions and providing endless purrs of encouragement.

Oh, and also to my wife.

CHAPTER 1

"You know, I bet he doesn't even know a thing about ghosts," Jack says to Lydia, his teammate, who is glaring at a soda vending machine.

"Come on," she mutters as the soda can she bought doesn't budge.

"He says he's psychic," Jack scoffs. "As if." He crosses his arms and watches people rush around with their luggage. "Why do we even have to add him to the team anyway? I thought we were doing just fine on our own. I mean, come on, you know—you've been on the team for years. We've identified plenty of paranormal activity without a psychic tagging along, right?"

"Uh-huh," Lydia responds distractedly. "Hey, can you shake this for me?"

"What?" Jack looks over and sees her trying and failing to jostle her soda out of the machine. "Won't that just shake it up?"

"Better than losing another dollar." Lydia delivers another kick to the side of the machine. "I've already lost four!" she yells as if the machine can hear her and is holding her drink hostage just to spite her.

Jack grabs either side of the vending machine and rocks it back and forth. "Shaking vending machines is pretty dangerous, actually. You know, I read that something like 13 people die every year from this."

"Shake it faster, then. I don't want you to die before I get my drink," she jokes.

"Hey guys. Trying to steal?"

Jack turns to see their other teammate, Ferris Huang, standing behind them with their arms crossed and a stern expression. Jack and Lydia are about to object but Ferris cuts them off.

"Say no more. Allow me." They push up their sleeves and kneel in front of the machine, reaching a skinny forearm into its belly and pulling out a can of 7Up. They bow their head and offer it to Lydia. "Your Highness."

"Oh, I was trying to get a Diet Coke, but—"

"Shhh... You're welcome," Ferris whispers.

"Where's Adeel and Austin?" Jack asks.

"They're still by the escalators waiting for Cecil."

Cecil. That name already makes Jack grit his teeth and he hasn't even met him yet.

Ferris notices Jack's expression and says, "Oh, please. Lydia, is he still on his 'I hate psychics' crap?"

"Yep."

"Jackie, you've gotta get over this. He's coming on the house-calls tour no matter what you think. Might as well try to be okay with it. I am," Ferris says.

"Yeah, but you're okay with everything," Jack says.

"It's called cruisin' through life, my man. You should try it."

"Yeah, we're laid-back, my friend," Lydia says, cracking open her 7Up. "Life is just a little easier for us." Foam fizzes up and runs onto the floor. "Crap."

"Hey guys!" their teammate, Adeel Sahni, says as Jack, Lydia, and Ferris approach. "Austin, the others are here!"

Austin Miller, their webshow's producer, is facing the escalators. He turns and smiles at them. "What's up? Whoa, Ms. Clarke-West, you're looking pretty rough."

Lydia glares at him, but Jack agrees. The front of her overalls is covered in 7Up, and every sticky step squelches on the tile floor of the airport.

"Has he landed?" Ferris asks.

"Just a few minutes ago. He should be coming down soon," Austin answers. He turns to fully face the team and Jack notices the sign he's holding: *Mr. Cecil Cooper.* No one has ever held a sign like that for Jack, and he's met people at the airport plenty of times.

Austin pushes his glasses up by the edge of the angular frame. (He once admitted to Jack years ago that he doesn't really need them, but wears them when he wants to look sophisticated. Jack wonders why he's wearing them today.) "Now, I don't want anyone messing this up. Cecil is a guest"—he eyes Jack—"and will be treated as such."

Jack rolls his eyes. "I just don't get—"

"Why we're adding a psychic for the tour? Yeah, we know you aren't too into the idea," Austin says, and the others chuckle at the understatement. "It'll be good for the show. Give him a chance, Jack."

The show Austin is referring to is The Ghost Checkers, a paranormal investigation webshow. They don't have anyone on the team who can actually get rid of ghosts, so they just check for them. Austin says that's what Cecil is going to do; during their upcoming tour of house-calls to reportedly haunted homes, Cecil will be using his psychic abilities to banish ghosts in addition to the team simply confirming their presence.

Jack, who is actually grounded in reality, knows there is no such thing as psychics. In his entire career of paranormal investigation, he has never encountered a single ounce of evidence pointing to any self-proclaimed psychic having a mental connection to the paranormal. Multiple times, in fact, the Ghost Checkers have investigated a home that has been previously cleansed by a psychic, only to find that the entity is still present and just as strong as before.

"There he is!" Ferris says. They were the only member of the team who was already familiar with Cecil's YouTube channel, so it's natural that they'd be the one to recognize him.

Jack looks toward the escalator and glances from person to person until he spots a crown of golden curls atop a smiling, freckled face. Cecil has already spotted them and is waving vigorously. He steps around the couple in front of him and makes his way to the bottom of the escalator and heads toward them.

"Hello, Ghost Checkers!" he calls in a southern accent, arms thrown out wide, bags on the floor.

"Hi, Cecil!" Ferris calls back and runs up to meet him. They instantly lock into an animated conversation, gesturing at each other's outfits (Ferris in mostly black with enough chains on their belt to sustain a prison, and Cecil in a jaunty blue sweater layered over a bright yellow collared shirt. He looks like a preppy nightmare). They hug, and Lydia joins them. Cecil says something too quietly for Jack to hear and all three of them start laughing.

Austin walks over and Cecil reaches up to wrap him in a tight hug, a wide smile on his face. Overly familiar, in Jack's opinion.

Jack catches himself glaring and consciously mellows out his expression. He knows his pronounced brow and deep-set eyes can make him look like a 'crazed serial killer' as Ferris puts it.

Adeel pats Jack on the back and says with his usual amount of optimism, "Give him a chance. Who knows? You might like him!"

Then Adeel heads over to introduce himself, and Jack is left alone watching his friends fawn over a man who does nothing but lie.

Jack sighs. He wishes he were like them, ready and eager to believe in a little bit of magic. Instead, he's cursed with the knowledge that everything that exists can be quantified, measured, and understood. While that helps him experience the world closer to how it is, it also rules out any possibility of seeing the wonder in things.

He really does prefer it this way, though. Jack would rather lose a bit of magic but know when he's being lied to. And he knows he's being lied to.

Adeel moves a bit to the right and it's enough for Cecil to spot Jack where he stands a few yards away.

"Get over here!" Cecil says and gestures for him to join them. "Don't be a stranger!"

Jack hesitantly walks over and reaches out a hand for a handshake. "Jack Finch."

Cecil bats his hand away. "No handshakes here, Jack Finch. We're about to be teammates for the next couple o' weeks!" He yanks him down by the neck and hugs him tightly. "That's hug-worthy!"

He lets him go and Jack quickly straightens.

Cecil laughs. "Look at his little red face! Sorry if that was too forward, Jack Finch." Cecil sticks out a hand this time, and says, "Cecil Cooper. Psychic medium, and honorary Ghost Checker."

Jack shakes it with a grimace. "Pleasure."

The six of them climb out of Austin's red minivan and head into their hotel. After Austin checks in at the front desk, he assigns the rest of them to load luggage onto a cart. When Jack turns to follow them back out to the car, Austin catches him by the shoulders and walks him further into the lobby.

"So," Austin begins, "I know you're not too happy about Cecil joining the group. Do you wanna talk about it?"

"No, I don't want to talk about it." Jack is silent for a moment, then launches into, "It's just— Okay, so we all know psychics aren't real, right? I mean, it's all a gimmick. It's a lie. And adding him to the group just for publicity?" Jack shrugs off Austin's arm and turns to face him. "Come on."

"Jack, it's not just for publicity, exactly—"

"Then why? Are we really that desperate?" When Austin doesn't reply, Jack asks again with a vulnerable waver, "Are we?"

Austin hesitates and lets out a breath. "Funbuzz is threatening to cancel the show."

Jack's eyes go wide. Funbuzz is the online entertainment company that produces their paranormal investigation series on YouTube. Getting canceled would be devastating. Revenue from The Ghost Checkers has paid all of their bills for the last several years.

Jack thinks back to their first large checks from Funbuzz. Lydia spent most of hers on dog clothes for her husky, and Ferris spent half of theirs at some sustainable clothing store. ("Yes, it's expensive but think of the *Earth!* Also, you can't tell me these pants don't look cool.") Jack thought he and Austin were the only ones who placed their money wisely in their savings, until he discovered Austin's out-of-control bobblehead collection. ("They're like my children, Jack. What was I supposed to do, leave this poor little guy on the shelf? See, he's shaking his head 'no.'") Regardless of how they each spent their money in the beginning, losing that income now would be disastrous to all of them, emotionally and financially.

Not only that, but cancellation would mean that the team would be either dispersed into other shows or fired outright. Jack knows these people, his best friends, only put up with him because they're teammates. If they no longer had to be in the same room together, there's no way they'd want to keep up communication with him.

"I was gonna tell everyone tomorrow. I didn't want to ruin this investigation, but yeah man. It's true." Austin pushes his glasses up his nose.

"What can we do?" Jack asks.

Austin gestures to Cecil who is trailing behind the rest of the team, laughing as they fight to get the unwieldy luggage cart in the door. "This wasn't random. We added Cecil because of his own internet fame. Plus, we were thinking that his ability to banish entities as a psychic would create some buzz around the show. He's getting material for his book too, but the main reason he's actually here is for our show." So they're just using Cecil for their own gain. Jack finds that a little more palatable. "Don't tell anyone yet, okay, man? Let me tell them."

Jack nods, watching as Cecil puts on Lydia's pink backpack that had tumbled off the cart. This guy is supposed to save their show and their livelihoods, huh? Jack will believe it when he sees it.

"So Cecil," Ferris begins from their spot on the hotel room floor. It's evening now, and everyone is sitting around one of the suites. The golden light filters in through the windows and makes the red half of Ferris's split-dyed hair glow. "How did you find out you're psychic?"

Cecil replies, "Good question. Well, when I was about seven, I actually predicted my mother's next pregnancy. That was the first message I ever gave. Definitely a weird day."

"I bet," Lydia says, starstruck, twisting a lock of her long hair around her finger.

"Do you ever get random messages for people by accident? Like strangers?" Adeel asks from the kitchenette. His popcorn starts popping and he jumps.

"Yes, and I do share them. One time in college, I was on a date with a cute boy from my econ class and, oh my lord. We were at dinner and I suddenly got a message from his uncle."

"No!" Lydia says, eyes wide.

"Yes!" Cecil laughs. "And in the middle of our date I informed him that his dear uncle Louie thought his film degree was useless." Cecil holds up his hands innocently. "Louie's words, not mine!"

The group laughs and the conversation shifts to bad date stories, and Jack tunes them out.

His attention shifts to Cecil, sitting with his legs crossed beside Austin and Lydia. He's smiling as he looks between Ferris and Adeel who lightheartedly bicker with each other. Cecil laughs and—of course his teeth are perfect. Why wouldn't they be? Everything else is.

Austin's arm stretches across the back of the couch. He cracks some joke and Cecil laughs harder than it was worth. He pats Austin on the knee good-naturedly, but his hand lingers a little too long. Austin notices the touch and glances at Cecil with a smile. Jack watches as his smile sticks when he turns his attention back to the group.

Jack looks at Lydia and sees no concern on her face. He glances at Ferris, then Adeel as he returns from the kitchen, and all of them seem to be having a good time. How can no one else see this? How are they all so utterly caught up in the con?

But Cecil will help their view count. Even Jack can admit that. When he first found out Cecil was going to be joining the group, he did a deep dive late one night. Cecil's YouTube channel *Coopernatural* is surprisingly popular, with over 4 million subscribers. Jack scrolled through video after video with hundreds of thousands of views, most featuring other YouTubers Jack has never heard of but he assumes are equally famous or more so.

Jack could only bring himself to watch one of Cecil's videos, but it was likely representative of the rest of his content. It was with a YouTuber named Krissy K. The video began with the two of them sitting on a couch together introducing their respective channels. They were lit up brightly, their ring light visible in the reflections in their eyes. Cecil asked her a few questions, scribbled on a piece of paper like a kindergartener, and told her about her dead uncle's affair in Vietnam. For whatever reason, Krissy K started crying, a single, perfect tear sliding down her cheek. Then Krissy K told the viewers that the other half of the collab would be on her channel where she and Cecil would make slime together. Whatever that means. Jack did not want to find out.

But the views on Cecil's video don't lie: a reading with some random YouTuber garnered over 5 million views. Even Jack will grudgingly admit if anyone is going to get their views up, it's Cecil. But Jack doesn't have to like it.

"Right Jack?"

He's ripped out of his thoughts by Lydia, who looks at him expectantly. "Yeah," Jack says, praying he didn't just agree to something terrible. The rest of the group seems satisfied with his answer, though, and the conversation moves on.

Jack stares at Cecil, who laughs along with the team and cracks his own jokes here and there. How obnoxious. Jack tunes back in when he hears them start talking about fraud. This should be interesting.

"No," Adeel says, shocked.

Cecil says, "Yes, the whole internet really did think I was a fraud in 2016."

"No!" Adeel insists.

"Yes! I did this giveaway when my channel started to grow, and this lucky lady won a free reading. We did it as a livestream, which seemed like a good idea until I started getting all the details wrong. Turns out I was channeling my own mother, not hers. Needless to say, the internet latched on and would not let go, saying it was staged and didn't go to plan, calling me a 'grief vulture' and saying I just try to profit off people's losses. Obviously that's not true." He pauses and rubs a hand down his cheek and across his chin. "That's part of why I'm wanting to release a book. Get some new, positive press out there. Only problem is, I don't know what it should be about. That's part of why I'm here—to figure that out."

Of course he's using them, too. Cecil is supposed to be *their* pawn, not the other way around. Jack glares at the wall.

Adeel tosses empty soda cans into a plastic bag, ties it up, and sets it next to the trash. (He always insists the hotels will recycle if he gathers up their recyclables and no one has the heart to tell him otherwise.)

Cecil says goodnight to each team member and walks out the door, headed to his own suite.

As soon as the door closes, Lydia turns to Jack and says, "What the fuck, dude?"

Jack looks at her questioningly.

"You were glaring at everyone all night. What is your problem?"

"Seriously, man," Ferris speaks up. "It was weird."

"I'm in a bad mood," Jack explains weakly.

Lydia scoffs. "Well, yeah. I figured that out for myself."

"I don't know what you want to hear. I guess I'm not a 'Coopernaturalist'." Jack hates that he knows the name of Cecil's fans.

"But why? What has he done in the four hours you've known him to make you hate him so much?"

Jack chews his lip and looks down.

"Jack," Austin says, and Jack glances up at him. "You know we love you. You're our lead investigator—"

Lydia coughs.

"—one of our lead investigators, and we of course want you happy and comfortable with any changes we make. But buddy," Austin says, sitting on the arm of Jack's chair. "You've gotta work with us here. Why don't you like him?"

Jack thinks for a moment and takes a breath. "I just don't like it when people lie."

"Jack." Austin cocks his head and sighs. "You don't think you can try to just... I don't know... give him a chance?"

"He's really nice," Adeel adds.

Jack looks at him with disbelief.

"Okay," Austin starts, "I can tell we're not gonna convince you. But Cecil is going to be part of our group during the tour. Hopefully you can find a way to be okay with that."

After patting him on the back, Lydia and Austin head to their own suite, and Adeel makes his way into the bedroom and claims the bed by the window. Jack watches as Ferris gets comfortable on the sleeper sofa.

"Was I really being that awful?" Jack asks.

Ferris stops violently fluffing their pillows and looks over at him. "Um..." they consider his question, their finger on their chin. "Yes."

Jack groans. He might actually need to get this in check.

Jack is pulled from his dreams by rolling thunder. He doesn't remember seeing that on the forecast. It almost sounds like breathing... Oh. It's just Ferris's god-awful snoring. Jack glances at the alarm clock on the table between the beds. It reads 3:00 AM. He glances over at Adeel laying on his stomach with one leg hanging off, toes grazing the mottled brown hotel carpet.

Jack rolls onto his side, but it isn't long before his arm goes numb. He sits up and shakes it out, then tries sleeping on his stomach before his neck protests. Jack turns onto his back and throws his arms out, huffing out a frustrated sigh. He stares up at the ceiling, the curtains allowing the slightest bit of light past them, throwing long shadows from every little bump. Jack studies them, hoping to be drawn back into sleep, but his eyes stay open and his mind stays buzzing.

Jack turns on his side and screws his eyes shut. Frustration creeping in, he's suddenly reminded of his nights spent trying to sleep during his childhood.

When Jack was seven, he and his father moved into his aunt's house in Florida to help take care of her after she got sick. The house was where Jack's father, Keith, and Jack's aunt, Mel, grew up. Jack saw his first ghost there.

It was a man in a dark suit, and he would walk across Jack's room every night from the closet to the opposite wall and disappear. Jack began to know him as the man in the suit.

Sometimes he would appear simply as a shadow, sometimes a fully formed specter, but Jack would see the man in the suit nearly every night, no matter how hard he tried not to open his eyes.

Jack doesn't know why, but it took him a long time to tell anyone about the ghost. After a few weeks of poor sleep, his aunt fussed over him nonstop, following him into the kitchen to ensure he was eating enough and making him special teas to help him sleep until Jack finally caved and told her about the entity. As soon as she learned about the man in the suit, Mel called Jack's grandmother, Hattie, who dropped everything to come down from New York.

Jack turns over in the lumpy hotel bed and remembers the night the three of them sat awake in his room waiting for the man in the suit. Jack's grandmother was lightly snoring, Mel was sleepily playing solitaire on the top bunk, and Jack was sitting with his back against the wall clutching his stuffed rhino. He began to doze off but caught a glimpse of a shadow. "It's there, that's him!"

The two ladies sprang into action. Mel climbed down as Hattie demanded to know why the spirit was in the house. Mel gasped and began speaking as the spirit in a low voice.

Jack remembers how scared he felt, how tightly he clutched his rhino, how small he tried to make himself in the back corner of the bottom bunk.

His aunt and grandmother seemed to successfully banish the spirit, but he never wanted to feel that fear again, feel that uncertainty, his body shaking, eyes as wide as they'd go, his hands clutching his rhino so hard he could pop its seams.

In the morning, he told his father about their banishment of the spirit. Upon discovering this was the true purpose for Hattie's visit, he was livid.

After speaking to the two women in the other room, he took Jack aside and told him that that was not the correct way to deal with a spirit. He told him that in no circumstance would he ever have to contact a spirit directly. "You can always rely on what is measurable, Jack. The more you understand, the less afraid you will be. Anything can be studied and understood. Okay?"

Jack nodded his head, eyes still wide and hands still wrapped tightly around his rhino. His father looked at him sadly for a moment before taking his hand and leading him into the garage.

Jack's father rifled around in a few boxes before finding what he was looking for. "Here we go," he said as he handed a small black box to Jack. Jack turned it over in his hands and looked up at his father questioningly.

"This is an EMF meter. It can sense energy in the air and tell you when it changes. That means there might be a ghost present."

"Cool," Jack breathed, extending the antenna.

"I made this myself when... Anyway, it's yours." Jack's father smiled tightly and placed a hand over his son's. "Listen to me. You do not ever need to contact a spirit." His eyes grow strangely serious. "I don't want you ever to contact a spirit."

Jack nods.

"That was scary, right? Before, when they talked to the man in the suit?"

Jack nodded his head.

"Mm-hmm. That's because you didn't understand what was going on. The unknown can be scary, Jack. It really can. But the man in the suit... He can be measured. He can be understood." He gently took the EMF meter from Jack. "Take a look."

The rest of the evening, Jack's father taught him how to use it, and that night, he slept in Jack's room while Jack slept in Mel's. The next morning, he emerged from the room and said simply, "It's gone."

Mel had turned to Jack and whispered, "You're welcome."

Jack never saw the man in the suit again.

Jack turns over one more time and breathes deeply. Austin asked why he disliked Cecil. Simple. When Jack sees him, he hears his father's words reminding him that no spirit ever needs to be contacted, ever *can* be contacted. When Jack sees him, he sees someone who claims to do what none should even attempt.

Jack knows half the world doesn't believe in the supernatural in the first place, but Jack's belief in ghosts is a rare constant in his life. He has studied and observed all he can about spirits, and he has successfully stamped out the fear from his life.

To study and understand is to do away with fear. But it goes the other way, too; what can't be understood terrifies Jack, though he would hate to admit it. Jack can't study Cecil's connection with the dead, if it even exists, so he isn't able to stop fearing it.

Jack takes a deep breath and settles into the bed. His last thought before drifting off is of what his father was going to say. Jack wonders for the thousandth time what his next words were going to be, why he made the EMF meter in the first place. Maybe he'll finally ask him one day.

The next morning, Jack is the last to wake up for once. He finally sits up with a start when Ferris tosses a pillow onto his face.

"Come on, man. Ghosts await."

Jack gets ready in record time and the six of them head out to the van. Lydia calls shotgun a split second before Ferris does, so they race each other to the passenger door, Lydia winning by a hair. Ferris climbs into the middle row behind her, and Austin takes his place in the driver's seat. Jack realizes with a sinking feeling that depending on where Adeel sits, he may have to squeeze into the back with Cecil.

"Hey," he grabs Adeel's arm and asks, "Where are you sitting?"

Adeel looks at him with wide eyes. "Why do you want to know?" he says slowly. "Did you do something to one of the seats?"

"No, I just—" Jack starts, growing frantic as he watches Cecil climb into the back row of the van.

"Jack, stop harassing the intern," Austin calls out the window.

Adeel shrugs Jack's hand off and quickly walks to the van and takes the last center row seat.

Jack grits his teeth and follows. Ferris hops out to allow Jack to climb through. Jack looks at them pleadingly and Ferris, practically the devil, smirks at him and shakes their head. Resigned to his fate, Jack grudgingly climbs into the back seat with Cecil.

Austin sets out for their next house call, and Jack looks out the tiny triangular window to his right. The roughness of the road is evident back here, and he and Cecil bounce with every dip, Jack's head almost hitting the ceiling each time. He clutches onto the seat belt stretching across his chest and keeps his eyes firmly on the houses flying by.

"So," Cecil begins. "Sleep well, everybody?"

There is a chorus of affirmative answers from the team.

"How about you Jack? Sleep well?"

Jack glances over at him. "Yep."

"Really? You look a little tired."

Jack could scream.

CHAPTER 2

When they arrive, it's a little after 4 PM. They pull around the corner and into the driveway of the house and as soon as Ferris hops out, Jack rolls their seat up and escapes the car, flinging himself out onto the concrete, feet barely catching him in time. Once out, he takes in the house in front of him.

It's a small cottage-like house with vibrant flower beds in front of the two large windows on either side of the blue front door. Above the old timey mail slot, there is a lion door knocker. Lydia walks up to it, lifts the heavy bronze ring, and knocks it against the door twice.

Jack glances over at Adeel, who is already filming. Ferris has their enormous tech bag slung over their shoulder, and

Austin and Cecil stand a few feet away from Lydia at the front door.

It flies open and reveals a young couple.

"Hello!" the woman says excitedly, but the husband smiles tightly, and Jack doesn't miss the way it morphs into a grimace.

"Hey folks, how's it going? I'm Lydia, one of your lead investigators. Can we come in?"

The couple opens the door wider and everyone files into the house. Jack walks in last.

As soon as he enters the home, his jaw drops. The home is decorated nicely, it looks tidy enough, but Jack can't stop his eyes from widening.

Every flat surface is decorated with porcelain dolls. Adeel pans his camera around the living room, capturing every dainty face.

Just as Jack thinks he has adjusted to the hundreds of pairs of tiny eyes, he makes the mistake of looking up and jumps. There are two enormous clown dolls suspended from the ceiling.

"You have a lovely home," Austin says with a nervous smile. The team introduces themselves, and Jack learns that the couple's names are Angela and Michael. He would know this if he ever read Austin's debriefs.

"Coffee?" Angela offers and walks into the kitchen.

As soon as she leaves the room, Michael says quietly, "Sorry about all the dolls. They're kind of her thing."

"How many are there?" Cecil asks.

The husband lets out a tired sigh and says, "Hundreds. And they're all named."

Jack sees Ferris shudder next to him.

"Here we go," Angela says, returning from the kitchen. She hands out coffee as Jack wanders to a curio cabinet filled with smaller dolls. The smallest is around an inch tall and its eyes stare deep into his soul. Jack feels goosebumps raise on his arms and his blood seems to pick up a chill. How can someone live like this?

"Alrighty, folks," Austin starts. "So, let's start out with an interview, we'll find out what's been going on, and we'll get some footage of the house."

The couple nods and they sit together on the small loveseat. Cecil and Lydia sit down across from them on the other couch and Jack takes his place in the armchair. Ferris trains their camcorder on the couple, and Adeel focuses on Lydia and Jack while Austin stands out of frame.

"So, Michael, Angela, how long have you lived in this home?" Lydia asks.

"Not long, actually. We've lived here for maybe four months."

"And you're already suspecting the presence of a paranormal entity?" Jack asks a little too loudly, surprise in his voice. Generally, families take a few months to even acknowledge something paranormal is going on.

"Well, from the first night, actually," Michael says. "We had put up about a third of the dolls already, and in the middle of the night, we heard them falling off the shelves, one by one. We thought we had a rat running around knocking them over or something, so I got up to check, but then—"

"Georgina!" Angela cuts in. "My dear Georgina fell off the wall. Not even a shelf. She was mounted to the wall in a place of honor, and she was just thrown to the ground. Her head cracked, and I did my best to fix her, but she'll never be the same."

Lydia says, "So an entity manipulating the physical space. That definitely sounds like an extreme case. I'm glad you called for us."

"We didn't know what else to do."

Lydia turns to Adeel's camera and says dramatically, "We're going to do what we do best and check this home. After that, if we determine there is an entity present, Cecil will work his magic and rid the home of its energy. Let's get started."

Ferris, having grabbed their folding table from the van and set it up in the middle of the living room, begins preparing all their gadgets. They hand mic packs to Lydia, Jack, and Adeel, then distribute various sensors and meters. Jack takes his favorites: an EMF meter and a temperature scanner. He prefers these because they provide the most concrete, specific information.

Austin stands speaking with the couple, explaining when they can return to the home. Angela stands next to a suitcase with her jacket draped over one arm. The conversation ends and she turns to her phone, but Michael looks around, eyes wide, a bead of sweat forming at his temple. He spots Jack and starts walking over. Oh no. Jack knows that look: a man with a secret to tell. Jack tries to walk away in time, but Michael catches up to him.

"Hey, man, can I tell you something?" *Ugh.*

Jack opens his mouth to respond but Michael talks over him.

"It was me," Michael admits.

"Uh, what?"

"I'm the one that..." he lowers his voice even more and continues, "broke Georgina."

Jack nods slowly.

"You don't get it, man. Living around all these dolls... It changes you. I was just filled with this *rage...*"

"Okay."

"And now you guys probably think it's a demon or something, and I just don't know what to do."

"Well, you can start by relaxing. We're going to investigate the home exactly as we always do, and whatever we find will be accurate. Don't worry."

"I didn't mess it all up?"

"No."

Michael nods, and before Jack can dodge, Michael pulls him into a hug. He whispers in his ear, "Thank you."

"Uh-huh." Jack untangles himself and steps backwards, and Michael joins Angela by the front door. They wave goodbye before walking out.

The team continues preparing for the investigation while Jack wanders around the house. He counts two bedrooms, one bathroom, and a few linen closets but stops when he remembers seeing another set of windows towards the back of the house when they were driving up. He opens the door to one of the linen closets again and places his hand against the back of the closet. It shifts under his palm, so he pushes harder, and it swings open. He steps over the pile of extra toilet paper on the floor and enters what appears to be another room.

Jack stops dead in his tracks at the sight. In the middle of the otherwise empty room there is a wooden chair. Perched on the chair is a doll with a cracked face.

Jack hears a noise behind him and spins to face it, relieved not to see an entity, nor Cecil.

"Hey, what—whoa." Lydia pauses in the doorway when she spots the doll. "What..."

"I think that's Georgina."

"Freaky."

Jack nods. "Freaky."

Lydia zooms in on the doll and pans around the room. She has always been the better of the two of them at getting footage. Jack prefers to experience it through his eyes, not a camera. Austin used to talk to him about it in the early days of the group when it was just the two of them, but he quickly learned how stubborn Jack can be and took care of most of it himself. Jack has always been a bit of a thorn in Austin's side, even from the start, but everyone who met them during the humble beginnings of the group agreed there was some kind of magic between them.

Austin actually didn't like Jack very much at first. Jack knows most people don't. He has a pretty cold demeanor and can suck the fun out of a lot of things, or so he's been told.

About three weeks into making the show, Austin's dog needed emergency surgery on his eyes, and the only specialist who could do it was three states away in Louisiana. There was no way Austin could afford the travel expenses, let alone the vet bill.

But Jack had just recently received his inheritance from his grandmother. She loved animals more than anything and instilled in Jack that same compassion. The money was just sitting there in his bank account, not doing any good for the world, so he gave it to Austin.

Austin rejected it immediately, saying he didn't need Jack's money, that he didn't need Jack's pity, but Jack insisted, saying it's not pity, and that Jack had always wanted to go to Louisiana anyway. (Austin still doesn't know Jack used to go every summer and hated it.)

They roadtripped up there together and got Austin's dog the care he needed. Their late nights in the hotel were the spark for the current format of The Ghost Checkers. Sure, their budget was nonexistent, but they proved to themselves they could survive on ramen packets in low-cost motels, and most importantly, they could survive each other.

Austin was the first person in Jack's life to really give him a chance. He wonders if Austin knows how much he means to him. He should tell him.

Jack is pulled from reminiscing when Lydia says, "Let's go let the rest of the team know. This thing is creepy." Oh yeah. There's a terrifying doll staring at him. Right.

Lydia leads them back out of the room and into the living room where Ferris has finished turning on all the sensors and is dialing in the live feed on the tablets.

"Hey guys," they say.

Lydia ignores them and skips straight to: "Guys, creepiest doll in the world officially spotted."

"Yeah?" Adeel asks from behind his camera. "Sick."

"Super sick," Lydia agrees.

"Okay, let's get a shot of Cecil exploring and finding the doll. Where is it, Lydia?"

"Well, Jack's the one who found it. It's through a false back in a linen closet."

"No way," Adeel breathes.

"Alright, Cecil, go ahead and 'find' that doll. Ferris, if you wanna follow him..."

After the team passes and heads down the hallway, Jack sighs and drops his head back. These theatrics will be the death of him one day. He takes a deep breath and follows them.

Cecil opens the linen closet and places his palm against the back just like Jack had. "Hey, Lydia," Cecil says, "Look at this." He pushes the door open and looks at Lydia with his eyebrows as high as they go. Even Jack can admit he's really selling it.

Cecil waits for Ferris to catch up and get a good angle before stepping into the room with the doll. He gasps and brings his hands to his mouth. Jack rolls his eyes at the acting. So over the top.

"Oh my god," Cecil says, choked up. It sounds pretty real, and Jack looks over.

"What's going on?" Lydia asks.

Cecil steps back toward her and reaches out his hand to grab her shoulder. He whispers something to her, and she replies, panicked, "Okay, that's okay." She looks at Austin who is peering into the room and waves at Ferris to stop filming.

"What's the problem?" Austin asks.

"That doll is—Oh, this probably sounds so silly," Cecil says, wiping his cheek.

"No, go ahead, Cecil."

"That doll is... It's so sad."

"Are you kidding?" Jack asks, immediately growing upset.

Cecil looks at him with wide eyes and opens his mouth to reply.

"You're supposed to help us raise our views and you can't continue the show because the doll is too 'sad'." Jack says mockingly.

"Jack—" Lydia starts, but he cuts her off.

"No, this is ridiculous." Jack takes his mic off from around his neck and shoves it into Ferris's hands. "Grow up," he says to Cecil harshly before walking back into the living room. He knocks a doll-themed pillow onto the floor and sits down on the couch. Jack leans forward and lets his head drop into his hands and takes breath after shaky breath until he starts to calm down. He drops one of his hands to rest over his knee while he props his forehead on the other. When did his anger get this bad?

A few minutes later Lydia walks into the living room, spots him, and storms over. "What the fuck was that?"

Jack looks up at her and chews his cheek.

"We were rolling," she says. Jack opens his mouth to argue that Ferris had stopped filming by then, and she cuts him off, reading his mind and saying, "*Adeel* was still rolling. That could have been usable footage, even great footage, if you hadn't let your ego get in the way. Just because someone else can hunt ghosts too doesn't mean it's a personal attack on you."

"But he can't hunt ghosts, Lydia."

"What are you talking about?"

"Did you see how he was acting? That was the fakest thing I've ever seen. And you guys were loving it. It's ridiculous."

"He was not faking. After you stormed out like a pre-teen, he started crying, Jack. Crying. Real, actual tears. He told us that the doll is attached to an entity, and that the entity is distressed. Cecil feels everything entities feel. Did you know that, Jack?" When he stays silent and won't meet her eyes, she bats him on the shoulder and repeats, "Did you?"

"No."

"I didn't think so." They stay quiet for a moment, Lydia glaring at Jack as he refuses to meet her eyes. She lets out a breath and sits down next to him, reaching to pick up the doll pillow Jack had tossed to the ground and laying it in her lap. "I know you didn't know that." She picks at a frayed hole on the edge of the pillow and sighs. "Why is this so hard for you, man?"

Jack sighs and sits back. He chews his cheek again. After a long moment, he says simply, "I don't know." He pauses and adds, "I mean, I do know. But it's not like he's lying to people on purpose, I guess. At least, I don't think he is. He probably really does believe in all this stuff." Jack sighs. And if Cecil really thinks he's being genuine, he must really think Jack's an asshole. "I'm sorry, Lyd."

She slings an arm around his shoulders. "It's okay, man. Just try and keep it together, okay?"

He reaches up and pats her hand. "Will do."

The rest of the team walks into the living room and Cecil pointedly avoids glancing in Jack's direction, eyes red. Jack feels a twinge of guilt. Sure, he has some big criticisms of psychics, and sure, the very sight of Cecil makes Jack's blood boil for all the people that have been tricked, but maybe it's possible Cecil really believes in it himself.

"You feelin' okay, Cecil?" Austin asks quietly, rubbing Cecil's back. Cecil leans into the contact and Jack scowls at the lack of professionalism. What happened to Austin? He used to be such a stickler for decorum.

"Right as rain," Cecil replies, not shying away from the proximity.

"Good." Austin glances out the window at the darkening sky. "We'll start our nighttime walkthrough in a bit. 'Til then, sit tight." Austin walks over to the tech table and asks Ferris a question.

Cecil walks over to the couch and sits down on Lydia's other side.

"Oh, what's that, Austin? Be right there!" Lydia jumps up and flees the awkwardness.

"So," Cecil begins, but Jack cuts in.

"I'm sorry I reacted that way. It really seemed like you were just being dramatic." And he clearly was, but Jack doesn't want to get into that right now.

Cecil holds up a hand. "No, I wasn't looking for an apology. I was going to tell you I have a message for you. From someone I believe may be your grandmother."

If Cecil's act with the doll was ridiculous, this is ten times worse. Bringing up his dead grandmother? Is he for real?

"She reached out to me yesterday, and I know you aren't a big fan of mine, so I wasn't going to bother you with this, but seeing how you were acting back there... You clearly need some advice."

Jack scowls. "Are you joking?"

"I am not."

Jack glares at him for a moment, then says, "Fine." If Cecil wants to solidify Jack's hatred of him, he can go right ahead.

"She told me to tell you... that if you do not change your ways and accept things as they are, you will lose something very dear to you by the eighth stop of this tour."

Jack nods his head and processes that information for a few seconds before blurting, "Bullshit."

"Excuse me?"

Jack doubles down. "Bullshit." Cecil looks offended and starts to speak, but Jack cuts him off. "Psychics aren't real, that message isn't real, and my grandma's alive." That last part is a lie, but Cecil doesn't need to know that.

"Maybe an aunt then."

"My aunt is still alive, too." That's a good reminder to call Mel, however. She promised him she was well enough for him to leave on the tour, but that doesn't stop him from worrying about her, even if she is with his dad for the time being.

"I don't know what to tell you, pal." Cecil says haughtily. "I got a message from someone who knew you well and knows you need help. Listen to it or not. I don't give a care." Cecil waves his hands and stands up, joining Austin, Ferris, and Lydia at the tech table.

Jack sees Adeel by himself peering into the curio cabinet, so he joins him.

"Hey," Adeel greets him.

Jack smiles, then studies the dolls with him. There are several in various poses displayed around the case. Little plastic ones like Barbies sit in chairs. A couple clowns with articulated joints are posing as if waving to each other. A family of dolls sits on a mini picnic blanket.

Jack sees Adeel's reflection in the glass, and he doesn't look afraid at all. Instead, he just looks curious, not a drop of judgment in his eyes. Jack smiles imperceptibly and studies Adeel's reflection, noticing his stubble growing in around his jawline, and two little lines branching off of each eyelid where his eyes pinch when he smiles. He looks a lot older than when they met when Adeel was 19 even though it's only been, what, a year?

Jack has always liked him, ever since Adeel's first day interning on the team when he lost his balance and knocked over a 400-year-old haunted bust. But when it broke open and turned out to be hollow, they realized it wasn't a centuries-old haunted artifact. Even though he freaked out at first, Adeel actually saved them a lot of trouble because they were able to identify the bust as a fake right away and move on. He's been a welcome member of the group ever since.

"I like this one," Adeel says, pointing to a small doll in a mini rocking chair.

"How come?"

"She looks so peaceful."

Jack glances over at him and cocks his head. "Okay."

"Almost nighttime, team. Let's suit up," Austin calls out.

Lydia dons her night vision headset, Ferris hands Jack his mic pack again, and Adeel grabs his camera. Cecil cracks his knuckles like an idiot.

They do their walkthrough like normal, Lydia jumping at any noise and playing up the fright for the camera. Jack does no such thing. Jack knows Lydia is their viewers' favorite investigator, but Jack prioritizes authenticity above showmanship. He glares at Cecil as that thought crosses his mind.

They don't encounter any energy spikes outside of the doll's room, so after doing a sweep of the house, they reconvene at the entrance to the linen closet.

"Cecil, are you good to enter the room again?" Austin asks from behind them.

"I'm good, Austin."

"Right. Let's have you go through the door, and everybody else, follow him in."

They do, and as soon as they're all in, Adeel closes the door behind them. Even Jack jumps just a little.

The silence in the room feels inescapable, and the darkness seems to weigh on them. Every shadow swims in Jack's periphery, forming monsters and specters that disappear when he glances straight at them, dissipating back into his imagination.

"Ready, y'all?" Cecil asks. They nod. Cecil approaches the doll and kneels in front of it. "Hello... Dorothea. Is that your name? You need to leave this doll and leave this house." Cecil clutches at his chest and gasps. Lydia reaches out but he waves her off. "I'm good, I'm fine. That's how she died. She's showing me. Dorothea," he says to the doll, "you need to leave. I am sorry this happened to you, but you need to leave this family alone." He gasps again and puts one of his hands on the ground.

Jack glances at his meters and notices they're fluctuating wildly.

"Dorothea," Cecil grits out. "You need to leave." He cries out, but a moment later, opens his eyes and stands up shakily. Jack glances down at his energy meters again and is confused to see that they're back within normal range. He feels himself frown unconsciously, reeling at the coincidence. As soon as he becomes aware of his expression, he reverts it back to neutral. He glances at Ferris, making sure they didn't catch him going 'crazed serial killer' again.

"Are you..." Lydia starts. Jack looks around and sees how traumatized the rest of the team looks. Adeel has lowered his camera, but when he meets Jack's eyes, he realizes, and focuses it again.

"I'm good, sweetheart," Cecil says to Lydia. "She's gone. But boy did she put up a fight." He laughs despite their alarmed looks. They walk out of the room and Adeel closes the panel behind them.

"That was *amazing!*" Austin exclaims. Jack stares out the passenger side window. (Lydia sits behind him seething that he called shotgun first.)

"It's nothing, y'all," Cecil says humbly from the middle row. He's right; it *is* nothing. He just walked into a room and talked to a doll. "All it is is telling 'em to go when you need 'em gone." *Oh, please.*

"So cool," Lydia says, her rage over having to sit in the back seat apparently having dissipated. "And you learned all that as a kid?"

"Yes, I did, my dear."

"Awesome," Adeel says from the very back.

Jack clenches his jaw. Cecil has these people wrapped around his finger.

The rest of the way to the next hotel they listen to Ferris's weird cyberpunk hypnowave techno music. Jack is fairly certain that that isn't the right name of the genre, and that they will never give them the AUX cord again.

Though their rooms aren't suites this time, this hotel is even nicer than the last one. In the lobby, there is a piano that's set to play by itself. Lydia had filmed it and captioned it '*even ghosts are more talented than me*' with a sad face.

"See you all tomorrow morning?" Austin asks and everyone confirms. Because of the way the beds worked out, Jack has his own room at this hotel, and he happily heads down the hallway toward his peaceful sanctuary.

After setting his bags down, Jack flicks the lights on and takes in his hotel room. It has a double bed in the center with a small desk by the window and air conditioner. Jack reads for a while, working through an alien romance. He notices how cold the room is, and gets up to turn the air warmer, but the knob is stuck. Jack turns it harder, tries pushing it, tries pulling it, but it doesn't budge. Why can't anything just go right? Jack kicks the side of it like Lydia had done with the soda machine, but just like then, it does no good. He sits back down on the bed and tries to ignore it.

He clears his throat a few times, the air conditioning drying him out, and decides he'd like to live it up and spoil himself with some ice water, so he grabs the ice bucket and heads to the noisy machine halfway down the hallway.

While walking back, he sees Cecil duck into Austin's room. Immediately his blood boils at the sheer lack of professionalism. He knew that hug in the airport was too familiar for strangers. And the way they were sitting on the first day? Jack knows exactly what's going on in there. He listens at the door for a moment, but when he realizes it's a little too soundproof, he knocks boldly.

Lydia opens the door and—Lydia? Jack pushes past her into the room and what he sees is not exactly what he expected. Austin and Cecil are sitting on the bed together, which would be incriminating if Ferris weren't sitting between them with a bag of chips, if Adeel weren't standing at the microwave making popcorn, and if a movie weren't on the TV.

"What's going on?" Jack asks. Why is the whole team hanging out without him?

"Hey, Jack, uh..." Austin rises from his place on the bed, grabs their empty ice bucket, and walks over to him. He puts his arm around Jack's shoulders and says, "Come get some ice with me, buddy?" Jack holds up the bucket of ice he had just gotten, but Austin says, "Come on, walk with me."

Jack follows him into the hallway. "What were you guys doing in there?"

"We were reviewing footage from today."

"Your computer wasn't even open. Were you guys just hanging out?"

Austin stops and sighs. "We needed to decompress, and with you and Cecil in the same room... there's not much peace."

Jack stares at a scuff on his shoe.

"So," Austin says, walking toward the ice machine. "About earlier."

Jack's stomach sinks. "Yeah."

"You already know what I'm gonna say, Jack. That kind of behavior isn't what the Ghost Checkers stands for. I know you know that."

"I know. I just—"

"Hey, you don't have to explain. I know that wasn't you." Austin stops and faces Jack. "But you know that can't happen again." He takes a breath, then says, "If you can't accept that Cecil is part of the group for the time being, if you guys can't get along, well... The group is going to have to make a decision."

Jack sighs and nods. "Okay. I understand."

Austin claps him on the back and says, "Knew you would, buddy. Come on, ice is around the corner."

"I know," Jack mutters. He chews his cheek as Austin fills the bucket with ice. The word 'accept' has him stuck. Cecil said that he needs to accept what is, or lose something dear. Austin basically just said the same thing. That's a pretty compelling coincidence, but clearly, it's just that: a coincidence. Jack has no problem following Austin's directions, so he will accept Cecil as part of the team and do his best to get along with him, and that may seem like heeding Cecil's warning, but he's definitely not. He doesn't 'give a care', just like Cecil said. That may be the one thing they can agree on.

CHAPTER 3

The next house call is only an hour or so away. It's an old two-story Colonial-style home with ornate molding and a wraparound porch. The siding is painted a dark blue, and the trim is stark white.

The door opens as soon as Lydia goes to knock, and a gaunt man who can't be younger than 90 gingerly steps out onto the porch.

"Hello, folks," he says, voice scratchy. "Come on in." He opens the door wider and shakily walks back inside, gesturing for them to follow him.

"Are you Ernest?"

"That I am," he says, turning slowly to face Lydia. "And who might you be?"

"I'm Lydia, and this is Jack, Cecil, Ferris, Adeel, and Austin. We'll be helping you out today. I hear you have a spirit present? We'll be able to both check for its energy, as well as get rid of it for you. Any questions?"

The man is silent for a moment, then lifts his hand to cup his ear and says, "What?"

"We're gonna get rid of your ghost."

"Yes, I need that."

"Would you like to sit and tell us about your experience?"

"Let me get us some tea first. Please, have a seat." He gestures to the large sofa and loveseat in the sitting room.

Lydia, Jack, and Cecil find seats while the other three stay standing to film. Lydia ties her long hair back without a hair band which will always both astound and terrify Jack.

After a few minutes in the kitchen, the man comes back with mugs and a teapot clinking in his shaky hands. He sets the mugs down on the coffee table and begins to pour the tea, but spills some on the table. Jack supposes, because of the man's shaky hands, the possibility of getting him to draw a sketch of the entity is not in the cards.

"Here, let me," Cecil says, then gently takes the teapot from the man and begins pouring for him.

Jack can't help but think of his aunt. Her tremor has gotten worse in the last year or so. He has to pour her drinks fairly often, and despite his dislike of Cecil, his heart warms a bit at the sight.

"So, sir," Cecil begins. "What have you been seeing?"

The man sits in one of the chairs and is quiet, gazing into the middle distance. He would look like a wax figure if not for the steady rise and fall of his shoulders. Jack is about to try to get his attention again when he finally speaks. "I see my wife."

The hair on Jack's arms immediately stands on end and it feels like the breath has been sucked out of him. Jack glances at his teammates and they seem to feel the same way.

"I'm so sorry for your loss," Cecil says.

"And to be clear, you do want us to clear her energy from this house, right?" Lydia asks.

"I don't know if she even knows she's here. She doesn't seem herself. She just drifts. Does that make sense?"

"That's pretty common, actually," Jack says. "Very few entities are really sentient. Some just relive the way they passed, over and over." Jack sees distress cross the man's features, so he quickly explains, "Well, 'relive' might not be the right word. The spirit you see is more... energetic residue. The core of your wife isn't still here, just part of her energy."

Ernest nods his head.

"Where does she manifest?" Lydia asks.

"At the top of the stairs most nights. She just stands. Or hovers."

"When did it begin?"

"Only a day after she died. That's how I know it's her," he pauses, "since I can't see her face."

The team pauses. "Why can't you see her face?" Lydia asks carefully.

"There isn't one."

Ferris gasps quietly behind the camera.

Lydia asks a few more questions before they wrap up the interview.

"Oh, and one more thing," Ernest starts as they stand up. "Will it hurt her? When you get her to leave?"

Cecil answers, "Absolutely not."

"How do you know?"

Cecil thinks for a minute. Wordlessly, he stands and walks to his backpack lying next to Ferris. He returns with a pad of paper and a pen and sits back down.

"What are you doing?" Jack asks, confused, but Cecil ignores him.

"Ernest, I have the ability to interact with those who have passed on. I like to scribble on paper because it helps me tune in to them. That's what this is for." He gestures to the pad. "Would you like me to contact your wife for you?"

Ernest says, "That would be nice, yes."

Manipulating this old man who is clearly still missing his wife? Jack shakes his head. Despicable.

Cecil begins scribbling on the page in wide circles and squiggles. Soon he nods his head. "Your wife, was her name Rosemary?"

Ernest's mild expression masks his shock fairly well, but it's clear in his eyes. "Yes."

Jack squints, then glances around at his teammates, but none of them look skeptical. How did Cecil know this man's wife's name? It must have been on the debrief. Jack never reads Austin's debriefs, so that makes sense.

"She's showing me a heart and a lock," Cecil continues. "Like a lock and key. And a bridge. Do you know what that might mean?"

Immediately Ernest's eyes start to redden, and when he speaks, his voice is tight. "We traveled to Paris a few years ago. We knew it would likely be our last trip together, and she had always wanted to go to Paris, so I finally said okay. She knew about this bridge where you can put a lock that symbolizes your love, so we did." He chuckles. "I thought it was kind of silly but she told me that that lock meant we'd never be apart. I guess she was right." His eyes drift toward the stairs. Jack glances at the dark stairwell, shadows pulling away from the wall, the chill of them reaching Jack where he sits in the living room. He rubs his hands over his forearms.

Jack has no idea how Cecil guessed that. He frowns at the ground. There's no way he really is psychic... right? No way that message he gave Jack could have been real? Jack shakes the thoughts out of his head. No, of course not.

"I can tell you right now that her spirit, soul, essence, whatever you'd like to call it— it's only present in you, not in the ghost you've been seeing. So, when we clear that energy, we won't get rid of the part of her that stays with you, only, as Jack put it, her energetic residue."

Ernest nods. "Did she say anything else?"

Cecil scribbles for a moment more, then says, "Only that she loves you more than anything." Cecil smiles sadly at him, a tenderness in his eyes.

Austin gestures for Ferris to cut, and steps closer to the rest of them. "Alright, sir. We're going to step out for a while, get some dinner, and be back to do our walkthrough and energy clearing. We'll see you soon, okay?"

They say goodbye to Ernest, then climb back into the van.

"Where's dinner?" Ferris asks.

"Where do you think?" Austin says. Jack groans. Wendy's.

Now, after a horrendously greasy meal and with the sun low in the sky, Ferris and Adeel are setting up the tech table. Ernest has already stepped out for the evening. Jack is standing near the front door, zoned out with his eyes on the staircase.

Cecil startles him when he says, "Is she up there?"

Jack glances down at him. "No." Does Cecil not have eyes?

"Maybe soon, though, huh?"

Jack doesn't reply.

After a moment of silence, Cecil says, "Why are you so rude to me?"

Jack looks over, surprised.

"Since the first day I've been here, you're all glares and shrugs and grunts. It's like talking to some meathead quarterback from high school. And as far back as I can remember, I haven't done a thing to you." Cecil stares at him as Jack stays quiet. "Have I?"

Jack glares down at him out of the corner of his eye. "No."

"Then why are you acting this way? I haven't done anything wrong."

Jack scoffs and smiles bitterly. Is Cecil really pretending that lying to their faces about his 'gifts' isn't wrong?

"Jack. Will you look at me please?"

Jack turns to face him directly and raises his eyebrows.

"I'm trying to talk this out with you."

Jack's challenging expression softens. "I know." He sighs. "Cecil, look. I'm sure you're a fine guy. But psychics... I'm never going to be able to suspend my disbelief for that. Sorry."

"So you're saying I'm a fraud?"

Jack raises his eyebrows again and looks away.

"Unbelievable." Cecil stomps away. Jack sighs again and his shoulders drop. Maybe he should be a little nicer to the guy. Cecil was right—it's not like he's done anything to Jack personally. Well, aside from hoodwinking his friends.

"Alright, folks," Austin says, gathering the team around. "We've got an active non-sentient entity that manifests at the top of these stairs." He gestures and everyone looks to the dark stairway. "The homeowner has confirmed we have full access to the home, so we can investigate the entire property. Let's have Lydia and Adeel take the bottom floor and basement, and Jack and Cecil, you two take the upper floor and attic."

Jack looks at Austin in disbelief, but Austin widens his eyes and nods pointedly.

"All four of you, come get your tech," Austin says.

The team gathers around the tech table as Ferris hands out mic packs, GoPros, and various sensors.

Jack bumps against Austin as he reaches for his temp reader. "What are you doing?" he says in a low voice, where only Austin can hear.

"You two need to learn to get along. Play nice," Austin says quietly.

Adeel grabs the large camera rig and trains it on Lydia and Jack.

"Today we are investigating a unique haunting," Lydia says. "This entity appears at the top of those stairs"—Lydia points and Adeel zooms in—"and has been haunting her surviving husband for years. The scariest part? The specter has... no face," she says dramatically. Jack stands awkwardly in the background with his hand shoved in his pockets.

"Uh-huh," he says flatly.

Adeel lowers the camera. "Jack," Adeel starts nervously. "Um, please don't take this the wrong way. I know I'm just an intern, and you totally don't have to listen to this, but—"

"Go for it, Adeel."

"If you don't have anything to add to the recordings, then maybe... just stay quiet?"

Ouch. Jack nods. "Okay."

"I'm sorry, that was way out of line."

"No, Adeel, you're good, buddy. I mean, you're the one who sees it from the viewers' perspective, so you have the best feedback. Don't worry about it, bud."

Jack is startled by Lydia crashing into him holding her phone. Jack realizes she's doing a livestream and groans internally. Jack hates livestreams.

"Jack, say hi to the people!"

"Hi."

Lydia turns toward him. "Once more, with feeling," she says.

Jack clears his throat. He waves his hand and says louder, "Hello."

"He's hopeless, you guys!" she says to the audience of the livestream. Jack sees the chat scrolling at the bottom of the screen next to the string of hearts rising up. One of the chat messages says, '*Where is his personality LMAO.*' Another says, '*look at his adorable little face oml lydia PROTECT HIM!!!*' Jack frowns. Why does he need protecting? Lydia leaves Jack for Ferris who immediately makes a peace sign and laughs. Some people are just suited for social media. Apparently Jack didn't get that gene. He watches Ferris and Lydia for a moment. Ferris's round, wire glasses gleam in the sun as they stand on their tip toes and wrap an arm around Lydia, both of them smiling and saying something to the camera. Jack finds himself smiling too. He has always felt

Lydia's smile is contagious, wide and toothy with freckles painting her cheeks. She has never liked her freckles, especially when they get darker and stand out more in the summer, but Jack's always liked them. He doesn't think there is anything wrong with freckles.

"Sun is down, people. I repeat, sun is down," Austin announces. "Let's begin the investigation."

Ferris and Austin stay at the tech table keeping an eye on the feeds while the two teams depart. Cecil and Jack walk up the stairs, and Jack doesn't miss how gingerly Cecil takes the steps, as if he's trying not to be noticed.

None of them have seen the entity yet, and the man's hands weren't steady enough to draw her appearance, so 'no face' is all they have to go on.

Jack sets his camera down on a small table by the top of the stairs and notices the way Cecil jumps at the sound.

"You okay?" Jack asks with a lopsided grin.

"Yeah, fine."

"Look, I know you aren't used to ghosts. Everyone would understand if you just decided to stay downstairs with Ferris," Jack taunts.

"You think I can't handle this?" Cecil says, insulted.

"No, I just want you to know it's fine if you decide you can't—"

"I *can*, Mr. Finch," he says sassily.

"Okay," Jack raises both his hands, a sensor in each one. "Just sayin'."

Cecil goes ahead of him, pointing his flashlight down the hallway. Jack can't resist— he creeps up beside him and flicks his fingers next to Cecil's ear. Immediately, Cecil ducks and runs halfway down the hallway. "Oh my god!"

Jack can't stifle his laughter, and as soon as Cecil hears, he whips around and stomps back over to him.

"Oh my *god*," he repeats, angry this time. "How dare you!"

"Sorry. I'm sorry." Jack wipes the tears out of his eyes. He is very much not sorry.

Jack picks his camera up off the table and turns it on, focusing it on Cecil who has resumed his path down the hallway. Looking through the viewfinder, in this lighting, Cecil's blond hair almost looks silver. He notices how his shoulders hunch inward, betraying his unafraid facade. Jack smiles subtly, so small that Cecil wouldn't detect it even if he were standing right in front of him. So small Jack can almost deny it himself.

Cecil comes up to a door and looks at Jack before pushing it open and stepping in. *No doll, no doll, no doll,* Jack hopes.

"Oh my god," Cecil says from inside the room, terrified. "Oh my god, Jack!"

Adrenaline fills Jack's veins instantly, and his heart starts pounding. He rushes into the room. "Cecil?"

He stops in his tracks when he sees Cecil standing in the middle of the room with a big grin on his face and his camera in his hand. Cecil doubles over laughing when he sees Jack. "Your face!" Cecil laughs.

Jack frowns. "You were messing with me?"

Cecil just laughs.

Despite himself, Jack feels his own face try to split into a grin to match Cecil's, but he fights it off. "Good one, I guess." Jack says, a smile still threatening him at the corners of his mouth.

"Great one," Cecil corrects him.

They continue their walkthrough, Jack's sensors lighting up at random. Nothing indicates to them that there is much of a presence.

Jack finds the attic entrance, pushes the cover aside, and unfolds the ladder. He shakes out his arms and lets out a breath. Attics are not really his thing. He climbs up enough to stick his head through and hold his temperature reader up.

"What do you see?"

"Nothing much." Jack starts to climb back down.

Then he gets a heat signature in the far corner.

"Oh, got something," he says to Cecil. "Not sure what it is." He shines his flashlight towards that corner and doesn't see anything. He shines it around the rest of the attic and just sees a few boxes and bins.

A box tips over and its contents scatter across the attic, marbles rolling toward Jack. They clatter down the ladder and Cecil yelps and jumps out of the way. Jack huffs out a laugh.

Jack looks at the screen of the temp reader. As the entity moves, he can make out its form and it's—just a rat.

He tells Cecil as much, and he nods, eyes still fixed on the entrance to the attic.

Jack pats him on the shoulder. "Don't worry. It won't hurt you," he teases. Cecil scowls.

They rejoin the group on the first floor, and Jack asks Lydia and Adeel how it went.

"Whole lotta nothing."

"Yeah, us too."

Ferris says, "Anyone wanna try the spirit box?"

"No," Jack answers immediately. He prefers measuring energy levels and collecting data, not pretending to communicate with spirits through a rigged radio.

"It's an important part of the investigation, Jack, you know this," Lydia says. "Plus, the viewers love it," she says to Adeel's camera with a grin.

"What's the spirit box?" Cecil asks.

Ferris shows him. "It's a little tricked-out radio that scans through radio frequencies very quickly. Sometimes syllables get through, but if enough syllables get through together to form a word or even a sentence, we can assume that it has picked up an entity trying to communicate. It would be too big of a coincidence otherwise, since it's scanning through frequencies so fast."

Cecil nods, clearly only partly understanding.

"All you need to know is spirits can talk through it."

"Got it."

"Let's set it up at the top of the stairs," Lydia suggests, and the rest of the team nods in agreement.

She walks gingerly up the steps and as soon as she's up high enough to reach, she leans and places the box on the top step before flicking it on.

It immediately begins emitting a pulsing, chugging static sound as it changes from frequency to frequency several times every second.

Adeel climbs to the top of the stairs and carefully steps around the gadget, training his camera on the box. Ferris points theirs up the stairs from the first level.

"Let's get started," Lydia says. She climbs halfway up and sits on a step. "Rosemary, are you here?"

She waits a moment, and a syllable comes through that sounds like, *no.*

"No?" Lydia repeats. "Who is this?"

Stop.

"Who are we speaking to?"

No.

Lydia looks at the rest of the team, seemingly at a loss.

"Let me give it a shot," Cecil says, climbing a couple steps. "Are you angry that we are here?"

Leave.

"You're not Rosemary?"

No.

Lydia jumps back in. "Are you the person Ernest sees at night?"

The spirit box is silent, and Cecil is about to ask another question when the spirit box says, *Yes.*

The group collectively shudders. If the faceless ghost isn't Ernest's wife, who is it?

"Why are you here?"

Home.

"You used to live here?"

Years.

"It's been years?" Cecil clarifies.

The spirit box is silent.

"Do you know that Ernest lives here now?"

Yes.

"Can you tell us your name?" Lydia asks.

The spirit box doesn't reply.

"What is your name?" Lydia asks again.

Still, it doesn't reply. They ask a few more questions without answers, so they assume the entity is done speaking to them.

"One-word answers. Very compelling," Jack says, crossing his arms.

"Yeah. It's like talking to you." Lydia elbows him.

"So," Austin begins, "let's get some shots of the house at night. Maybe some of the investigators creeping around. You know the drill."

Adeel and Ferris start filming B-roll around the living room. After a minute or so, Ferris walks over and says to the three of them, "Creep around."

Lydia takes the lead, shining her flashlight around the house. Adeel jogs to the upper floor to get a shot of her walking up the stairs. Cecil follows suit, leaning into the dramatics and creeping behind her. Jack stays downstairs, actually looking around for supernatural activity and entity manifestation, unlike certain investigators who live solely to be on camera. Jack knows that's not exactly fair, but he doesn't care right now.

The others get to the top of the stairs and begin 'investigating' the upper floor. Ferris is still on the lower floor with Jack.

Jack glances toward the stairs and his heart stops when he sees a dark figure at the top. He squints at it, thinking for a moment it could be a member of the team, but as far as Jack knows, all of them have faces. This dark figure has strands of hair falling in front of its cheeks, framing the area where its face should be. Where there should be eyes, flesh smooths across the sockets. Where there should be a mouth, there's nothing, just the faint imprint of teeth straining against the skin. It floats inches above the top step with its shoulders hunched forward. If it had eyes, it would be staring at Jack.

He grabs Ferris's arm and points toward the entity. Jack's breath catches in his throat and his muscles freeze as if any motion could disturb the incredible apparition in front of them.

"Whoa," Ferris breathes as he fumbles and frantically points the camera in the shadow's direction.

"Guys," Jack calls. "She's here."

The others scramble back toward the stairs.

"Where?" Lydia says as she walks forward.

"Lydia, wait—" Jack says as she steps right through the figure without even noticing. Jack's shoulders fall as their most compelling specter sighting dissipates into thin air.

"Tell me you got that," Jack says to Ferris.

Ferris grimaces as they check the footage. "I don't think it picked up quite right."

"What do you mean?"

"The room's a little darker on camera than it is in person. I guess I didn't have the settings right. You can... kind of see her. But it isn't very clear."

Jack places his palms on the back of his head and turns away, walking toward the kitchen. Why isn't anyone on this team competent at their jobs? Why can't a single one of them actually do what they're supposed to do? That was the clearest manifestation the team has ever encountered, and it's gone without a trace.

Jack lets out a strangled sound of frustration and leans on the kitchen counter. He chews his cheek as he pictures what his father would say. *That's what you get for making specters into spectacles.* He shakes his head, tossing his father's words out of his mind. He stands straight again and takes a shaky breath.

Adeel peeks around the corner with his camera. Jack can't even be mad at him because he's sure it was Austin who asked him to film him. Wordlessly, he shoves past him and back into the living room.

"Jack—" Lydia starts, but he interrupts her.

"Do your jobs," Jack says in a low voice. He doesn't miss the hurt that crosses Ferris's features, but he's so frustrated he can't bring himself to care.

"But—"

Jack holds up a hand and closes his eyes. "Just... do your jobs."

With that, he walks out of the house. He knows it's best to distance himself from frustrating situations, but he can't help but feel like a teen storming out. Guilt starts creeping up from his stomach to his throat.

As soon as Jack gets outside and takes a breath of fresh air, the anger starts to leave him. Before he even realizes what he's doing, he has dialed his aunt's number. The phone rings a few times before she picks up.

"Jackie?"

"Hey, Aunt Mel."

"What's wrong sweetheart?"

Jack opens his mouth to answer but all he can do is huff out a shaky breath.

"Oh, sweet boy. It's okay. Start from the beginning."

Jack sits on a plastic chair on the small porch and sighs. "Mel, I think I messed it all up."

"How so?"

"Well, okay, so we're on this house-calls tour right now."

"I know! I've been telling everyone I know. You know, my neighbor Sherry says her son-in-law's house is near one of the stops on your tour."

"Mel—"

"Oh, sorry sweetie. Go on."

Jack laughs. "I was gonna say, we brought on this guy—Cecil Cooper—and he's the worst."

"Oh, really? What has he been doing?"

"He's—" Jack struggles to find the words to describe just how awful he's been. "Well, he—I guess he... Okay, well, he's lying to all my friends. He says he's a psychic, but I know he's not, and they all think he is, and they love him. Mel, they're all obsessed with him. He can do no wrong."

"It sounds like they're paying more attention to the newcomer than you, even though you've been there for them since the start," Mel says. She never fails to understand him.

"Yes, exactly! And the fact that he's lying to them at the same time, it's just..."

"It feels unfair," Mel offers.

"Yes!"

"Have you considered that maybe he isn't lying?"

"Well, no, because—"

"Because psychics aren't real," Mel says, quoting Jack himself.

"Yeah. But that's not exactly all."

"What else is there, sweet boy?"

"I kind of..." Jack rubs the back of his neck. "I sort of blew up on them. A few minutes ago. They messed up this investigation and we could have gotten the best footage we've ever gotten, we could have even proved paranormal activity to the world, but they messed it up."

"Why do you think they messed it up?"

"Lydia was so distracted she walked through the apparition, and Ferris didn't have their camera set up right so we didn't get any usable footage of it."

"How did that make you feel?"

"Like I'm the only one on the team who actually cares about our work," Jack explains.

"Do you think that's related to how you're the only one on the team who didn't accept Cecil right away?"

"I mean... I don't know."

"That must be pretty lonely for you, huh? Being the only one who knows the truth and having nobody believe you?"

"I guess." Jack supposes it's pretty isolating, especially because there is nothing he can say about it without the team having to 'make a decision.'

"Don't you think he might feel the same way?"

Jack frowns. He hadn't thought of that before. Psychics aren't real, of course... but maybe Cecil *thinks* they are. Maybe he doesn't know he's lying. He probably does feel pretty lonely.

"You there, sweetie?" Mel asks.

"Yeah, I'm here."

"I love you so much, dear boy. I've gotta go. Are you gonna be okay?"

Jack smiles. "Of course, Mel. Love you."

Talking with his aunt is a surefire way both to feel exponentially better, and exponentially more guilty for not being there. Her kind words are sometimes all that can remove the weight from Jack's shoulders, and the smiles he can practically feel through the phone remind him there are better days ahead.

But there aren't a lot of better days left. Mel got sick when Jack was seven. For a long time, she was stable, but in the last few years, her illness began to progress again. Seeing her lose weight she didn't have much of in the first place, seeing the way she hid her pain made Jack unsure about leaving for the Ghost Checkers tour. His family is his priority, and he wouldn't leave town if she needed him, but Mel told him over and over that she's fine, that she'll see him when he gets back. Jack has a constant tugging in his chest that tells him she might not. *Accept what is, to change what will be*, she'd say. Mel has always connected with the Zen way of thinking and takes every opportunity to encourage Jack to let go of every little detail and allow life to flow the way it's supposed to.

No, thank you. Instead of letting go, Jack would much prefer to grab onto anything he can in life to ground himself and clutch it as tightly as possible until he feels steady on his feet. He definitely doesn't feel steady yet.

Austin appears on the threshold of the house. "Hey," he says carefully. Jack hates when they walk on eggshells around him, but he guesses he doesn't give them much of a choice when he blows up like that.

"Hey, Austin. Sorry about that, man. I was just frustrated," Jack rushes to explain. Austin had already threatened him once with kicking him out of the group. Jack doesn't want to see if he's bluffing.

"You're good, buddy. I talked to the team and they're sorry that the investigation went sideways. They all forgive you for your reaction. But *buddy*," Austin says, stepping closer, shaking his head, "you've got to get that anger in check. It doesn't look good on the other side of the camera, I'm telling you. Ferris and Adeel will edit this episode carefully, but I can't promise we can make you look good if it happens in the future. You could ruin a whole investigation with another outburst like this."

"I know," Jack says with a sigh. He wonders where that anger comes from, thrumming in his fingers, pounding in his chest. If he ever looks closely, he knows he might find fear hiding in each breath. "I know."

Austin pats him on the back. "Alright, brother. Let's get back inside, yeah?"

Jack follows him in and sees Ferris packing up the tech table. "We're leaving? But Rosemary—or, well..." he glances over at Cecil on the couch, Lydia sitting on the arm rubbing his back.

"Already done, my friend. She went without a fight as soon as she understood this wasn't the right place for her energy."

Jack nods, trying to look as impressed as the rest of them. He clenches his jaw.

"It was amazing," Lydia sings. "Seriously Jack, you should have seen it, I'm talking *amazing.*"

Jack laughs. "I bet."

He helps Ferris pack up the tech table and load it into the van, an unspoken apology and request for forgiveness, which Ferris accepts with a smile and a "Thanks, man."

Ernest returns home and the team finishes up the episode before setting off toward the next hotel. The whole ride there, Lydia and Adeel sing terrible karaoke and play road trip games with the rest of the team. On a normal day, Jack would be annoyed out of his mind but Jack just smiles, trying hard not to take these people for granted. He doesn't even mind sitting next to Cecil. Now *that's* progress.

CHAPTER 4

Jack blinks his eyes open as light suddenly floods the hotel room, pulling him from his dreams. He sits up and orients himself, sleepily looking over to where Ferris has ripped the curtains open.

"Up and at 'em, fellas."

Jack lets himself fall back down against the pillows and crosses his arms behind his head. Today is going to be different. He can feel it. He can taste it in the air. He can smell it in the—oh god, what is that smell? Jack glances over and sees Adeel peeling off his socks.

"Sorry, man," he says to Jack, tossing the sock across the room and into his suitcase.

It's no matter. Not even Adeel's ungodly feet can ruin today.

Jack steps out of the elevator with a smile on his face. "Good morning," he says to Austin as he passes him on the way to the sausage.

Austin stops in his tracks and stares at Jack as he passes.

Jack grabs a plate and loads up on links, biscuits, and gravy. He might even go back for a waffle. Anything is possible on this fine day.

"What's got you so chipper?" Lydia asks.

"I'm a changed man, Lyd." Jack sits at their table and digs in. He notices the team glancing at each other.

"Yeah," Lydia starts, "but *why* are you changed?"

Jack sits back in his chair and wipes his mouth on a napkin. "I realized yesterday, after my outburst..." he clears his throat. "I realized that life is precious. Why would I spend it so uptight? I don't want to waste the time I have with my favorite people." Jack squeezes Austin's hand where it lays on the table. "I've got a new lease on life, you guys." Jack resumes eating and says with his mouth full, "It's great."

"I bet," Lydia says, still suspicious.

"Well, I, for one, am proud of you, Jack. It's always better to accept things, isn't it?" Cecil says pointedly, referring to the message he gave Jack.

"That it is, Cecil. That it is." Jack smiles, but it doesn't reach anywhere near his eyes. He returns to his biscuits.

It would be impossible to change his uptight nature overnight, but Jack figures if he changes his behavior, his nature will follow along with it. Jack watched his Aunt Mel do the exact same thing when an awful woman named Marty had joined her bowling team. Mel pretended to like the woman just to preserve the peace within the group, but after a while of pretending, she came to genuinely like her. Jack figures he might be able to do that with Cecil. If that's what it takes to preserve the peace within his group, he'll do it.

And of course, this is not to enrich his life and better himself through positivity. This is purely to make it through the tour without losing his group. As Cecil said, he needs to accept things as they are, or lose something dear. That's not happening if Jack has any say.

The next stop in the tour goes off without a hitch. They find evidence of the spirit's presence, Cecil does his thing, and they're out of there, one more episode in the can. Jack is careful to show more character, too. That comment about his lack of personality on Lydia's livestream is definitely not one he wants to receive again.

After they get back to the hotel, Austin pulls him aside into the hallway. Jack can't help but think of the last hallway chat they had, but that time Austin had definitely not been happy. Jack's brow tightens as he wonders if Austin's onto his act, but Austin just stands staring at Jack, a dopey smile on his face.

"What?" Jack finally asks.

"Just taking it all in," Austin replies. Jack quirks his eyebrows, and the sandy-haired man explains, "This is the first time I've seen Jack Finch act so happy-go-lucky."

"What can I say? I guess I really took what you said to heart."

"So we're good?"

"We're good," Jack says.

Austin smiles, and with that, he walks into the hotel room and Jack follows suit.

His team members are sitting sprawled around the hotel room playing Mario Kart on the TV. Cecil has clearly just beaten Lydia who tosses her controller onto the bed and huffs out a sigh.

"Every time," she says.

"Wanna go again?" Cecil asks her, but she shakes her head.

"Just so you can absolutely destroy me one more time? No way, pal."

"Hey, Laid-Back Jack, do you wanna play?" Cecil asks, extending a metaphorical olive branch.

Lydia quickly answers, "No, he doesn't like—"

"Sure," Jack says with a smile.

Lydia gapes, eyes wide, and whispers, "Who *are* you?"

Jack sits on the bed next to Cecil and picks up the controller Lydia had discarded. Cecil laughs at him. "What?" Jack asks.

With a smile, Cecil takes the controller from him and turns it over before placing it back in his hands. "It was upside-down."

Jack smiles back at him. "Thanks." In this lighting, Cecil's hair looks golden. Why did he notice that? A frown flicks across Jack's face. Weird.

                    Connor Bryan

They play a couple rounds, Cecil absolutely obliterating him, and Jack being a good sport. He doesn't understand, though; he thought Mario would be the best character to choose. How did Cecil beat him with the baby version of the same character?

Jack gives his controller to Lydia, and she and Cecil play a round or two before Ferris groans, "I'm bored."

"Read a book," Jack deadpans.

Ferris looks at him blankly. "Read a *what?*" Ferris lets themself fall backward on the bed, then sits up on their elbows. "Lydia, do you want to steal a luggage cart and ride it through the hallways?"

"Is it really stealing if they're free to use?" Austin asks from the desk.

"It's stealing... if we keep it," Lydia points out.

"You can't keep it," Austin says.

"Ugh!" Ferris groans.

"How about a livestream?" Adeel suggests.

"Oh, how fun!" Cecil says. "I'd love to do a livestream with y'all."

"Okay, okay... Well, what should we stream?" Lydia asks.

"We haven't done a Q and A in forever," Adeel says.

"I'm sold," Ferris says. They throw a pillow at Jack who sits on the other bed. "You in, Jackie boy?"

Jack tosses the pillow back onto Ferris's face and says, "Sure." He knows he's on thin ice after yesterday, plus he's pretending to be Laid-Back Jack so if they want a livestream, it's a livestream they'll get.

"Alright!" Lydia cheers.

"Lydia, will you make the Instagram post announcing that we'll go live at..." Austin checks his watch and says, "10 PM? 20 minutes from now?" he asks.

"Sure." Lydia opens her phone and poses for a selfie, holding the phone up high and tucking her hair behind her ear.

"Really?" Austin deadpans.

"It's what the people want to see." She starts typing the post and sends it off.

Twenty minutes later, they sit down together, Jack, Lydia, and Austin on the couch with Cecil, Ferris, and Adeel in front of them on the floor.

Lydia sets her phone up on a stack of books and hits the button to start the livestream.

"What's up everybody?" Austin says excitedly. Jack doesn't understand how he has so much energy this late at night. "Tonight we're going to be taking some of your questions and we'll give you all the answers you crave."

What a gross way to phrase that. Jack wrinkles his nose.

Austin squints at the questions scrolling by. "Okay, okay—Lydia, since you joined the team pretty late, did you have trouble meshing with the rest of the group?"

"Ooh, that's a good one," she says. Jack agrees.

It's true that Lydia and Ferris were later additions to the Ghost Checkers. When Jack and Austin originally started as a duo back in 2016, they had no idea it would turn into anything. But only a year after they started posting videos, Funbuzz acquired them and drastically upped their budget. They were suddenly able to travel within a way larger radius, they could afford top-of-the-line gear, and they were able to quit their other jobs. (They both worked at a pet store, Austin in the fish department and Jack in rodents and birds. They were happy to stop coming home smelling like fish food and birdseed.)

It quickly became apparent they needed more people, however, so Funbuzz added Lydia and Ferris. Previously, they had both been working on a show called the 'Do Girls', where four women do various things for the first time. Lydia was in front of the camera, and Ferris behind it. When the Do Girls split up due to 'creative differences'—AKA, they discovered they were all getting paid different salaries—Lydia was plopped into the Ghost Checkers, and Ferris along with her. Neither had supernatural experience nor interest, but they quickly found their footing and became invaluable members of the team. The Ghost Checkers wouldn't be nearly as successful as it is today without them.

Jack looks at the rest of the team. In 2016, he had no idea some dumb YouTube channel would lead him to the best people he's ever met.

"Honestly," Lydia says, beginning her answer, "they were so welcoming." Lydia reaches over and grabs Austin's hand and reaches over him to grab Jack's. "These boys were my babes right from the start. I think I was only supposed to be comedic relief for the show, but as soon as I saw my first ghost with them, that was it. I was sold."

"Which was your first ghost, again?" Austin asks.

"The Moore Jail."

Austin and Jack nod. That was a good one. The old jail had been turned into a museum, and the employees kept seeing an inmate with clattering chains. Lydia ended up seeing him too. If Jack remembers right, she ran all the way to the van without looking back. It took her several more investigations to be able to film without her shaky hands ruining the footage. Jack chuckles at the memory.

"Okay, next one..." Austin looks for the next good question. "Are we taking more interns? Adeel, how long was your internship supposed to be?"

"Uh, one month."

"And how long has it been?"

"17 months."

Austin gestures 'there ya go' to the camera. "He's an internship hog." Austin laughs and says, "Nah, we love him. We don't ever want him to leave. But we don't really have the need right now for a second intern, so as long as we've got Adeel with us, no, we won't be taking on any more."

"One for Jack," Austin says. "Jack, what do you hate more—psychics, or demons?"

The team laughs, and Jack answers, "Well, neither is real..."

"We know, we know!" Lydia says.

"—but I guess I'd have to go with psychics." He knocks his knee into Cecil's shoulder.

Cecil comes back with, "What do you hate more: psychics, or having a personality on camera? It's hard to tell." Cecil turns his head and winks at Jack.

"Oh no he didn't!" Ferris shouts.

"Shots fired," Lydia says.

"Ouch," Jack laughs.

"Don't worry, I'll get you some water for that burn," Cecil says, and starts to stand up.

This is where it all goes wrong.

Cecil rises from his place on the floor, trips, and falls backwards into Jack, who catches him out of reflex. Cecil is laying across Jack's lap, back braced by Jack's arm, his hand wrapped around Cecil's shoulder. Jack's right hand panics, hovering over Cecil's knee.

It takes a moment for the team to register what happened. As soon as Cecil realizes, he scrambles out of Jack's lap and out of frame. Hands on his head, he mouths, *"Oh, fuck."*

Jack can't read every word on Lydia's screen from this far away, but he catches the comments in all-caps, which happen to be most of them right now. *'IS THIS REAL?'* and *'SOMETHING LGBT JUST HAPPENED'* are among them.

"Thanks for tuning in, guys!" Austin says hurriedly and ends the livestream.

Ferris slaps both hands over their mouth and says, muffled, "Disastrous... Catastrophic..."

"Jack, I'm so sorry," Cecil says, opening his phone.

Jack nods, still processing. "Maybe not many people saw?"

"The stream was at like eight thousand, I think," Lydia says.

Oh. That's not nothing.

Jack frowns and scratches his head. "Do you think they all noticed?"

Cecil shows him his Twitter feed which is currently full of people tweeting screenshots at him. Many are somehow already edited with a pink tint and heart emojis. In the photos which are conveniently cropped to look romantic, Cecil appears to be reclining into Jack's arms. Hm.

"I'm sorry, Jack," Cecil says, taking a step back and holding his phone to his chest.

Jack isn't seeing pink like the romantic filter; instead, he sees red. He closes his eyes and takes a deep breath, the thrum of anger in his fingertips receding. So their fans think he and Cecil are together. That's not too surprising to Jack. Fans of The Ghost Checkers are always overanalyzing their episodes and looking for relationships where they don't exist. Jack remembers how weirded out he felt when all the fans latched onto him and Austin just because they sat next to each other in an interview.

But this is different. While he has vowed to accept Cecil into their group to avoid more problems, he has not wavered in his stance regarding psychics. And for the entire internet to be convinced he's romantically involved with one? Hellish.

But it's not Cecil's fault. He didn't mean to fall into his lap. Jack looks at him and his big, worried eyes.

"It's fine," Jack says.

"No..." Cecil shakes his head.

"Really, it's fine."

"No, Jack, your phone—"

Then Jack's phone rings.

Shit. Of course Mel already knows. "One second." Jack walks toward the door to the hotel room and answers, "Mel,

I swear, there's nothing going on. It's just the internet being dumb."

The other line is silent for a beat before a man's voice says, "Jack?"

Jack's face goes cold and his eyes widen. "Dad," he says. "I'm sorry, I thought this was Mel."

"I just wanted to call and let you know your aunt had another dizzy spell today so she's at urgent care right now." As if he can sense Jack's growing panic, he immediately says, "But she's okay. She insisted that it's so mild it wasn't even worth telling you."

Jack leans against the hallway wall. "Okay," he breathes. "So are they doing tests or..."

"Yep, they're doing a scan and some blood work. She'll be fine, Jack. I just wanted to update you."

"Okay, thanks. Thank you."

They chat for a moment, compulsory small talk, before getting off the phone. Jack walks back into the hotel room and the rest of the team can immediately tell something is off.

"Is Mel upset?" Ferris asks.

"No, she's, uh... She's in urgent care right now. Dizzy again."

Austin nods and puts an arm around him. "You know you can always talk to us, bud. We're here for you."

"I know. I think I'm gonna go to bed you guys."

"Of course. It's late," Austin says.

Everyone who isn't sleeping in this room walks out with Austin, leaving Lydia and Ferris.

Jack sits on his bed and Ferris climbs onto it with him, wrapping their arms around him.

"I love you," they say, resting their cheek on his shoulder.

"I love you, too, Jack," Lydia says, hugging his other side.

Jack chokes out a laugh. "I love you guys too."

Lydia hops onto the other bed and Ferris gets the pull-out couch ready.

"That might have been the worst livestream we've ever done," Ferris says.

"Nope," Lydia corrects them. "Remember when Adeel's whole ass showed in the background that one time?"

Ferris falls over laughing. "No, don't remind me! Why was he even wearing pants that loose?"

Jack chuckles. He guesses this livestream could have been worse. Adeel could have forgotten his belt.

The next morning, the team is piling into the minivan when Austin says, "Hey, Jack, would you mind driving today? I've got a headache wanting to start."

Jack nods and climbs into the driver's seat. Austin used to get awful cluster headaches a few years ago that would knock him out of commission for days. Jack is used to driving when Austin's head decides he needs to rest in the back seat.

An hour or so into the drive, Jack hears snoring. At 12 PM. He glances over and sees Cecil in the passenger seat with his head back against the headrest and his mouth lolling open. Jack smiles, then remembers himself. He keeps his eyes firmly on the road the rest of the drive.

They arrive at the next hotel a little before dark. Jack pulls into the covered car loop and parks the van. Austin feels better by now, so he goes inside and checks them in.

Cecil stirs for the first time since they stopped at a rest stop a few hours ago. "What time is it?" he yawns, stretching.

"A little after eight."

Cecil nods his head, stretching his arms and looking around. "Are we in Virginia?"

"Yep."

"Last time I was in this state, I got booed off a stage."

"You what?" Ferris asks, leaning up over Cecil's seat.

"Yep. I was doing a live reading, probably eight years ago, that my manager pushed me into. I just wasn't ready for live energy work like that. I was so nervous. *So* nervous. And I flubbed it."

"You got people's info wrong like the livestream?" Adeel guesses.

"No, I was rude," Cecil explains. "I didn't have a filter yet, and I just reported every message I received. I—" Cecil begins, and interrupts himself with a laugh. "I told a lady her dead husband thought she was getting uglier with age." He covers his face with his hands as everyone laughs.

"Well, was she?" Jack asks.

Cecil covers his face. "She looked like a droopier Winston Churchill."

Jack chuckles.

Jack runs the luggage cart back downstairs to the lobby while everyone gets situated.

As soon as he walks back in, Cecil sits up and says, "Jack, Jack, Jack, Jack, it's bad."

"What's bad?"

"The fans' rumors."

"What about them?"

"They got to my *grandma*," Cecil says dramatically.

Jack just frowns at him, not quite grasping the gravity of the situation.

"My grandma," Cecil says slowly, pointing at his phone. "She texted me to ask about my new boyfriend."

"Oh." Jack nods slowly. "Who?"

"You!" Cecil says exasperatedly. He starts pacing with his hands on his head. "The rumors have gotten back to my grandmother, who believes them. *What?*"

"And that's bad because...?"

Cecil huffs. "It's not bad because of her, exactly, but they've spread so far they're getting back to people I know. It's getting a bit out of control."

"Oh. That's... troubling." If Cecil's grandma saw the rumors, who's to say they haven't reached Jack's own family too? He doesn't want to deal with the prying questions. He knows the harder he tries to deny it, the more his aunt would think it's true.

"Be back," Jack says, pulling his phone out of his pocket and stepping back into the hall.

It rings once before Mel answers. "Hey hon!"

"Hey Aunt Mel."

"How's my sweet darling angel boy?"

Jack laughs at the extended pet name. "I'm good. How are you? Are you feeling better?"

"Right as rain, my dear. Ugh, did your father tell you about my silly little dizzy spell? I told him it wasn't worth bothering you. I swear, I'll whoop some sense into him."

Jack laughs. That's very Mel.

"So why are you calling, honey?"

"Well, I was just wondering..." Jack pauses. How exactly does one ask if someone has seen a rumor without letting them know about the rumor? He tries, "Have you been on Twitter lately?"

"...Yes," his aunt says, growing suspicious.

"Okay. Um—Well. Anything interesting on there?"

"Like what, sweetheart?"

"I don't know. Anything about me."

"Oh, you mean like how my dearest nephew is in a committed relationship with a cute little YouTube psychic? Something like that?" she teases as Jack's stomach flips.

"...Yeah."

"Uh-huh, uh-huh. Well, if I *had* seen something like that, I would tell my dearest nephew angel baby that I think they make a fine couple, and that I can't wait to meet Cecil at Christmas."

Jack drops his head back and sighs. "It's just a rumor, Mel."

"That's what Bill Clinton said, and he got impeached."

"Mel, come on. There were rumors about me and Austin last year."

"You and Austin don't quite have the same electricity, dear. Oh, I'll talk to you soon, dear boy. Imani's here."

They say a quick goodbye and Jack steps back into the hotel room. He slips his phone back in his pocket. Jack has always liked Imani. She's been Mel's nurse for the last six or seven years, and he always appreciated how she would talk to Mel like an actual, coherent human being. Other nurses Mel had treated her as if she couldn't speak for herself, even though she was just as opinionated and well-spoken as she had always been. Imani was never like that. Jack smiles, glad she's being well taken care of.

When he walks back into the room, Ferris and Lydia are jumping on the bed and hitting each other with pillows like two pre-teens at a slumber party. "What the hell are you doing? One: we have downstairs neighbors who are probably trying to sleep, and two: you could hurt yourselves. Think." He snatches the pillow away from Ferris.

"R.I.P. Laid-Back Jack," they say, jumping half-heartedly.

"Hey, no, no, Laid-Back Jack is still here," Jack insists. "Not R.I.P." He hands the pillow back. "Hit each other. Go ahead. Not R.I.P."

Lydia flicks her eyebrows as if to say she doesn't believe him. "Austin, new entity to investigate: the ghost of Jack's fun side."

The house they pull up to the next morning is different from any of the others thus far. Usually they're old, a little decrepit, and clearly have had multiple generations of owners. This house looks brand new.

"That's weird," Austin mutters. Jack looks at him questioningly from the passenger seat, so he explains, "Well, it's just that when they submitted to the show, they said the specter is a little Victorian girl. I kind of expected an older house. More, I don't know. History."

Jack nods. He can already imagine the comments on the video saying the little girl is a demon. Jack makes it his mission to dispel the misguided idea that any kind of irregular entity can automatically be labeled a demon. Jack is a man of science, not superstition. He wishes more people were like him.

The homeowner, a red-headed woman named Shelly, welcomes them into the home and it's no less shockingly drab on the inside. It's decorated in the universal suburban style with western baskets mounted to the walls, random jars of olives and peppers on top of the cabinets, and a deep red accent wall in the otherwise slate gray room. Family portraits line the wall by the stairs. It's a nice house, but it definitely doesn't look like the dwelling of a little Victorian girl.

"So," Austin says to Shelly, getting down to business, "what makes you believe the spirit of a little girl dwells here?"

"Little *Victorian* girl," Shelly corrects him. "She leaves all the drawers open, she throws my crucifixes on the ground, she slams doors. The whole nine yards."

Jack asks, "Have you seen her?"

"Well, I had a dream about her. She looks to be about seven years old and wears this old frock-looking dress. Oh, and she has long dark hair that covers her face."

"Does she also have a twin she hold hands with at the end of hallways?" Ferris says under their breath, echoing what they're all thinking—bullshit.

Austin is slowly nodding his head, taking it all in. "Okay," he begins. "Well, thank you. We're gonna step out for a moment and start gathering our gear." He smiles politely at her, then ushers the team back out the door.

As soon as they're outside, Lydia says, "So... fake, right?"

"*So* fake!" Austin confirms.

Adeel looks puzzled and asks, "Why? Couldn't it be real?"

Jack answers, "Well, for one thing, this home is way too new for a little Victorian girl to be attached to it."

Ferris pulls up the property information on their phone and shows it to them. "Built in 2013. Before that, it was an empty lot."

"Native American burial ground?" Adeel posits.

"Nope."

"Well, then what is she seeing?" Cecil asks. "There could be *something.*"

"She's not seeing anything, remember? It was a dream," Jack points out. "She's only seeing the mess the spirit supposedly leaves. But if you look at any of the pictures they have hanging up, you'll see she has a son who looks to be about twelve. My guess? It's him."

"All of it? Even the crucifixes?" Cecil asks.

"Sure." Jack probably would have done it too if his aunt had those in the house when *he* was twelve. He's lucky Mel never subscribed to any specific religion.

"So what do we do?" Adeel asks.

"We investigate like normal," Austin says. "And when we don't find anything, that'll be her answer."

Adeel nods.

"Ferris, tech table, let's go."

With Adeel's help, Ferris sets up the table in the middle of the living room.

After Shelly leaves, Austin divides them up to investigate both floors, and having received their marching orders, they begin their walkthrough of the home, Adeel and Ferris filming. Unsurprisingly, their sensors stay quiet and the only heat signatures Jack picks up are of the team.

"Can we just go?" Ferris says. They're all certain they aren't going to find anything, but Austin shakes his head.

"Gotta be thorough. We're the Ghost Checkers. We've gotta check."

Lydia places a flashlight in the center of the floor in the kitchen. Jack has his EMF meter and temp reader on.

"If there is an entity, please turn on the flashlight."

Austin says, "Lydia, explain to the viewers what you're doing."

"So, if there is an entity in this house, she would not be tied to any structure or area. And the way she manifested to the homeowner in a dream would point to the entity never having been corporeal. Which means..." Lydia looks at Jack, who refuses to humor her. "Demon," she finishes. "A common way demons might show their presence is by flicking a light on or off. Something about that form of energy is just easier for them to manipulate."

"However," Jack begins with a finger in the air, and Austin rolls his eyes. "Demons are not confirmed to exist. In my professional opinion, they're simply irregular energy manifestations, not a malicious entity, and are not tied to any religious ideologies."

"We know, Jack," Lydia teases. She turns back to the flashlight and says again, "If there is an entity present, please turn the flashlight on."

As expected, nothing happens. Jack keeps his eyes on his meters, and they don't detect any energy.

Cecil elbows him and says, "Fat load of nothing, huh?"

Jack looks down at him and chuckles. "Fat load of rebellious son, more like," he says, and Cecil laughs.

"That was pretty astute of you, you know."

"Was it?"

"Yeah. I didn't think of that."

"Well, yeah. You're an amateur."

Cecil laughs as if Jack was joking.

Telling the homeowner that they think her spirit is actually just her messy, anti-god pre-teen goes about as easy as expected, but they do get some great footage of her cursing at them and telling them to get out of her house. For once, they're the ones banished from the premises, not the ghost.

Once back in the car, Austin sits back in his seat and says, "Did that just happen?"

Ferris says, "That was rough," and the rest of them agree.

"I was right," Jack says. "It wasn't—"

"Wasn't a demon?" Lydia says. "Uh, it was a pre-teen... so it kind of was."

CHAPTER 5

"Fifth stop," Jack hears from behind him. "You ready to face the consequences soon?" He turns to see Cecil lint rolling his purple argyle sweater. Cecil raises his eyebrows.

Oh yeah. Cecil's message. "There will be no consequences," Jack answers, turning back to the bathroom mirror to continue shaving, "because I have accepted things as they are."

"Have you?" Cecil asks. "That's great. What did you have to accept?"

Jack takes a careful swipe under his chin and rinses the razor as he says, "You."

"Me?"

"Yeah, you being here. It was pretty tough, too."

Cecil laughs and smacks him with the lint roller and it sticks. He walks out and Jack follows him with his eyes in the mirror.

Has he really accepted things as they are? He thinks back through the past few stops on the trip. Jack had had outburst after outburst. He'd never done that before Cecil joined the group. Austin had never had to threaten to kick him out before Cecil joined the group. Jack had never been so upset about fan theories before Cecil joined the group. Maybe he still has some work to do.

Jack peels the lint roller off the sleeve of his button up as his phone buzzes. He glances down at it. It's a text from his aunt: '*You can tell me anything, you know.*' He frowns at it and opens it, seeing the attached photo. It's a screenshot of the livestream at the moment Cecil tripped. Jack sighs.

He texts back, '*Nothing to tell, Mel. Just the internet being the internet like always*' and walks into the living space of the hotel room.

Jack will never understand why the team insists on hanging out in one room all the time. Austin is on the phone while eating a granola bar in the kitchenette, Lydia is braiding her hair, and Adeel is putting on new socks while Ferris is doing some kind of dance for him, their heavy belt chain clinking with every flailing movement of their hips. Their arms are outstretched high above their head and their fists move in a wide circle.

"See?" they say, out of breath.

"I mean, I guess it's bad, but I don't know if it would actually get you kicked out."

"Jack, we're trying to figure out if it's possible to dance so badly you can get kicked out of a club." Ferris resumes dancing and Jack can't help but laugh. He sits down on the couch next to Cecil, who sits with his knees up, nose buried in his phone.

"I'd kick you out," Austin says from the kitchenette.

"Thank you!" Ferris says, even more out of breath. "See, that's what I thought," they say to Adeel who shrugs.

"Do we have any actual work to do today?" Lydia asks.

"We did," Austin says, putting his phone in his pocket, "until the homeowners canceled on us."

"What?" That had only happened a small handful of times, and generally only after a not-so-good episode had aired. Jack thought back through their recent episodes and couldn't think of anything bad except for... oh yeah. His own behavior. Ferris and Adeel should have edited out his tantrum, but it's possible not all of it had been removed. Jack prays to no god in particular that today's stop hadn't been canceled because of him. If that's the case, maybe Austin should just go ahead and give him the boot.

Jack glances at Cecil. But it isn't the eighth stop of the tour yet. If Cecil is to be believed—and Jack doesn't know why he would believe him in the first place, but he entertains the idea for the sake of the thought experiment—then his unwillingness to change won't cause him to lose the group until the eighth stop. The homeowners canceling today's stop actually gives him a little more time, so maybe it's a good thing. Look at him, seeing the bright side. Maybe Laid-Back Jack really stuck. "Well, what should we do instead?" Jack asks.

"Clubbing!" Ferris shouts.

"It's 9 AM," Austin says.

"Morning clubbing," they whisper.

"Are there any museums around?" Adeel suggests.

"Maybe a dog park?" Lydia says. "You know I'm missing my Poppy," she whines, miming hugging her dog.

"Possible, possible..." Austin says, considering both their suggestions. "It'd be best to do something we could still get content out of so that today's not a total waste in that regard..."

"Ooh," Cecil says, sitting up, still looking at his phone. "There's the Virginia Museum of Hauntings and Curiosities!"

Immediately, everyone's eyes light up and if Jack wasn't already certain they're all in the right field, he definitely is now.

"We can for sure make a video or something out of that. When does it open?" Austin asks.

Cecil scans the webpage, then says, "Eleven."

"Do they have dolls?" Lydia asks.

"Probably."

"Haven't you seen enough haunted dolls recently?" Adeel asks her, and she shrugs.

"You can always use a haunted doll sighting to really wake you up, ya know? To shake your bones."

"Speaking of shaking bones, will they kick me out if I dance like this?" Ferris asks, busting out some terrible moves that look a bit more like flailing through a swarm of bees than dancing.

"Oh, most definitely."

They pull into the patch of dirt that serves as a parking lot. The building in front of them is exactly what Jack expected: a large Victorian mansion complete with creeping ivy and shuttered windows.

The team gets out of the van and follows Austin to the front door. He turns the knob and it creaks open.

"Awesome," Adeel breathes behind Jack.

They step into the entryway and see cobwebs hanging in the corners, sagging horror movie posters plastered to the wall, and a dusty chandelier.

Austin walks over to the front desk, but there is no one around. Jack walks up beside him and picks up one of the brochures for the museum and notices there are a lot fewer cobwebs in all those photos. He looks up again. Maybe they aren't just part of the gimmick.

Suddenly, a small, old woman appears out of nowhere. She wears suspenders and thick glasses that make her eyes look enormous. "Hello!" she says cheerily. "Welcome to the Virginia Museum of Hauntings and Curiosities! I'm Ethel. Do you have your tickets already?"

The team buys exorbitantly priced tickets, Ethel hands out maps, and they begin their walkthrough of the museum.

According to the map, the museum is laid out in three sections, each a different story of the home. The first story is full of haunted or cursed objects like rocking chairs, eyeglasses, and dolls (much to the team's chagrin, and to Lydia's excitement). The second floor is home to curiosities like taxidermy two-headed snakes, jars of weird beetles, and old medical devices. The third floor is dedicated to odd stories of wild events like bank robberies, serial killings, and assassinations.

Jack takes his time looking at each display and reading the informational placards that go along with each one. His museum style is much different from Ferris and Lydia's, who race from exhibit to exhibit in no particular order, just going to whatever catches their eye next.

They're already on to the second floor before Jack even finishes half the exhibits on the first. They've been to museums as a team before, and that's usually how it is; by the time Jack finishes, the rest of them are already in the car.

Jack finishes reading about a cursed egg spoon and joins the rest of them on the second floor where Austin and Cecil are examining a Jackalope head mounted on the wall.

"I don't think so," he hears Cecil say.

"Yes," Austin insists. "My cousins and I used to hunt for them every summer, I'm telling you."

"But did you find any?"

"No."

"Well, there you go."

They both laugh and move on to the next exhibit. Jack doesn't understand how they've gotten along so well since the first day they met. Jack could have sworn they were longtime friends when he saw the fond way in which they greeted each other at the airport a few days ago.

A few days ago. It's only been less than a week since this whole mess started. Jack remembers months ago when Austin first started planning the tour, and now they're almost halfway through.

Jack thinks back to that morning when Cecil reminded him the fifth stop is coming up. He bites his cheek and wonders if he has accepted things enough. Jack figures there's no harm in heeding Cecil's advice, right or wrong. If he's to be believed, Jack only has two more stops before fate takes over. Even though he's a man of science, Jack's stomach fills with lead. Losing these people would break him.

Jack glances around the room and spots each of his teammates. Lydia has grabbed Adeel by the wrist and is dragging him over to a six-footed goat skeleton. Ferris is entranced by what claims to be the world's largest taxidermy bat. Austin and Cecil are making their way around the second floor together, heading toward the stairs.

Sure, he's not the most natural on camera, and sure, he isn't one for showmanship. But he loves this job, and more than that, he loves these people.

Jack knows they could get canceled if their views don't improve. Cecil is there to improve them, but Jack can do so much more himself, too.

He follows the rest of the team up to the third floor and spends a while reading fascinating stories about lives incredibly different from his own. Jack has never told anyone this, but when he was younger, he used to want to be a bank robber. Now that he's an adult, he knows he shouldn't crave crime, but as a kid, he dreamed of the fast-paced, ever-changing life of an old-timey bandit. What happened to him?

Now he craves routine and an early bedtime. He guesses that's just part of getting older. And more boring.

Jack joins Adeel and Lydia by a cardboard cutout of a woman from the 40s. They're speaking quietly to each other, but as he walks up, he hears:

"—get all the glory. We could, too."

"But isn't that lying?"

"Aren't all the best stories lies? I mean, how much of this museum do you really think is real?"

Adeel glances around. "All of it?"

Lydia laughs at him. "You are so sweet, my dear Adeel."

"What are you guys talking about?" Jack asks.

"We," Lydia says, throwing an arm over Adeel's shoulders, "are cooking up a scheme. Tell him."

"Okay, so, first of all, I haven't said yes to it yet. But Lydia thinks it's unfair that—"

"That you and Cecil get the romance rumors and you don't even appreciate it! All press is good press, baby."

"So she wants to start rumors that she and I are together. For publicity."

"Adeel, you don't have to do anything you don't want to do," Jack says carefully.

"I know. But it's kind of a good idea. A scandal... It excites me." Adeel's eyes glint.

That's a side Jack has not seen before.

Lydia giggles and grins. "Are we doing this?" she asks.

"We're doing this."

They squeal and jump up and down. Jack finds someone else to talk to.

He walks around a corner and meets Cecil head-on.

"Jack! I wanted to show you this." Cecil grabs his wrist and Jack hopes he can't feel how his pulse jumps. Cecil leads him to an unassuming display case. All that's in it is a rusty crowbar, an old container of salt, and a bronze instrument with several different needles and gauges. Jack gently rests his fingers on the glass.

"Look," Cecil says, pointing to a portrait printed on the informational placard, "It's the first ghost hunter: Emmett Albright," he reads.

"Cool," Jack says, eyes eagerly taking in the old instruments.

"He practiced from 1864 to 1886. He's supposed to be the first paranormal researcher to publish his findings."

Jack nods. "Why'd you show *me*?" he asks, wondering why Cecil didn't drag the rest of the team over to see the display, too.

"Well, I don't know," Cecil starts. "He kinda reminded me of you. You seem like you take this the most seriously." He pauses, then quickly backtracks, saying, "Not that the rest of the team don't, I mean—I like them all, they're great at what they do but—"

"I understand. They're great," Jack begins, "but sometimes it feels like they're more into the YouTube side of our jobs than the paranormal."

"Exactly!" Cecil agrees. "You have the actual passion for it. I can tell."

Jack looks over at him and smiles. "Thanks, Cecil."

Cecil grins and looks back at the display. They stand there for a few more minutes, pointing out details to each other, Cecil cracking jokes and Jack actually finding him kind of funny.

They walk together from exhibit to exhibit. Jack doesn't tell Cecil he's already seen most of them on this floor.

Jack glances down at his phone and is shocked to see they've been at the museum for over three hours now. He looks over at Cecil, who is talking excitedly about some kind of pirate legend related to the cardboard cutout in front of them. Three hours and he didn't even realize. Jack smiles and looks back at the cutout of some swashbuckler he's never heard of. He could learn to like Cecil, he thinks.

Once they confirm with the map that they've seen all the exhibits, they head back downstairs where the rest of the team is sprawled across the chairs in the first hallway, clearly having been done for a while.

As soon as he sees them, Austin stands up and says, "Ready to go?"

"I'm so sorry, y'all, were you waiting long?" Cecil asks.

"Eh," Ferris says, standing and pulling Lydia to her feet. "No big."

Lydia smacks Adeel awake. "Come on, bud. Time to go."

"Oh, Austin, you wanted to do a video, right?" Jack asks, having totally forgotten.

"Already done, brother," Austin replies. "We got some sweet footage earlier. You and Cecil were busy, so we went ahead and made a couple TikToks."

The six of them thank Ethel and walk out to the van. The temperature has dropped by several degrees during the time they've been in the museum and Lydia shivers dramatically. As soon as Austin unlocks the doors, she scrambles in and starts chanting, "Heat, heat, heat!" and Ferris joins in. Soon, all six of them are chanting (including Jack, who feels the chill, too) and they all cheer as soon as Austin turns the temperature up.

"We're ridiculous," Austin laughs.

"But now we're warm," Ferris says. "Chanting works."

"What do you mean chanting works?" Jack asks. "Austin just turned on the heat. Dials work."

"Yeah," Ferris says, "but how did he know to turn on the heat?"

"Because it's cold and I'm smart?" Austin offers, but Ferris ignores him.

"Because we chanted. Chanting tells the universe what you want. Why do you think people chant at protests and stuff?"

"To tell legislators what they want."

"And they're part of the universe," Ferris points out.

"They're right, ya know," Cecil pipes up from the back. "Chanting is an ancient tradition. It works. I use it when I banish entities sometimes."

"A million dollars, a million dollars, a million dollars," Adeel chants.

"Nah, man," Ferris says. "It's gotta be something you really want."

"I do really want a million dollars."

"Do you want it in your soul?"

"Uh..."

"Exactly. It's gotta be a real 'I need this' kind of desire."

"Well, why are you the expert on chanting?" Jack asks.

"Because."

"Great argument."

"Silence, silence, silence," Austin chants. Jack silently seconds this.

CHAPTER 16

The sun is hanging low in the sky and orange light filters in through the thin curtains, gently illuminating the team as they lounge in various areas of the suite.

Ferris is laying on the bed with their head hanging off, looking at Cecil upside-down. They ask, "Cecil, do you ever contact pets?"

"Why, yes, Ferris, I do."

"Wait, really?" They sit up lightning fast.

"So if we went to a dog park..." Lydia begins.

"...You could contact all the dogs' ancestors?" Ferris finishes.

"Theoretically, yes," Cecil answers, opening his box of leftovers from lunch.

"That's so cool. Could you contact a living pet?" Lydia asks.

"Well, it's funny you ask," Cecil starts, "because this is the one thing I know I want to include in my book. This isn't something a lot of people understand about me: I completely believe in reincarnation."

Oh, please.

"What? But you talk to people *after* they die," Lydia says.

"Sometimes a long time after," Ferris adds.

"Yep, but what I am talking to is an essence of the person, not directly connected to their physical form. So someone can be reincarnated years before I contact them, and their consciousness is still able to come through."

"Wow," Adeel says in a whisper.

"So... you might be able to talk to Poppy? She's alive." Lydia asks.

"Theoretically... Is she a dog or a cat?"

"Dog."

"Okay, then likely yes," Cecil says.

"And you couldn't if it was a cat?" Jack asks.

Cecil laughs. "If it was a cat, ain't no way I'm getting it to talk to me." He turns to Lydia and says, "Do you have a toy or anything of hers?"

"I have her old tag on my keychain."

"Perfect!"

Lydia digs in her bag and pulls out her massive clump of clinking metal. It holds exactly two keys, and approximately 24 novelty keychains, including but not limited to: a shark-shaped bottle opener from Harry's Surfside Fish Fry, a foam stress-ball ghost, and a bisexual pride flag. She's a complex woman.

She finds Poppy's tag on the keyring and holds it out to Cecil, who takes it gently.

"Poppy," he reads. He holds the tag in both hands and closes his eyes. "Oh, a husky! I love huskies."

"Yeah!" Lydia confirms excitedly.

Cecil is nothing if not a good guesser.

"And beautiful eyes, oh my goodness. Two different colors."

"Yes!"

Jack frowns. That's pretty specific. He must have seen a picture on Lydia's Instagram.

"Okay, so she says..." Cecil laughs and says, "She loves you very much, but she also loves her pet sitter, Kim, because she gives her more treats." Cecil laughs. "Oh, she misses you so much, but knows you'll always come home to her."

With watery eyes, Lydia says, "Thank you, Cecil." She wipes her tears and laughs, "Oh my god. I can't believe you just did that. I didn't expect to cry on a random Thursday evening."

"Just doing my job, ma'am," Cecil jokes, handing Lydia's keys back to her.

Lydia gives Poppy's tag a kiss before tossing the clinking bundle back into her bag.

"Thanks, man."

"Don't mention it!"

Jack returns his attention to his book but fails to read any of the words on the page. An unshakeable truth Jack has known since childhood is that it's impossible for psychics to exist. But Cecil really sells it. It's hard not to wonder... Jack shakes his head. No. That's just too far beyond the realm of possibility. Right?

Jack glances at the team, each doing their own thing again. It was so easy for them to accept Cecil, even though they're all in the same field, and all presumably have the same evidence. Why can't Jack?

Because he's just a little more realistic, he supposes.

The team is quiet for a while until Austin yawns and says, "Why am I so tired? It's only 8 PM."

"We should watch a scary movie. That'll wake you up," Ferris suggests.

Jack takes a breath, ready to object, but Cecil lights up and says, "Oh my gosh *yes*! The chance to watch a scary movie with ghost hunters?"

"Ghost Checkers," Ferris corrects.

"Whatever. Sign me up!"

"Well," Lydia starts, glancing at Jack. "Maybe we should do it in the other suite. I don't know if Jack would be into it."

He smiles subtly at how considerate Lydia is. She may be a goofball, and she may give him some tough love sometimes, but deep down, she really cares. Jack glances at Cecil and sees how excited he is. Okay, maybe it's not that objectionable. "Actually," Jack starts, "I think it'd be okay to watch it in here."

"Well, I don't want the noise to bother you."

Jack makes a face. "Noise? What do you mean? I'll be watching it with you."

"Oh!" Lydia gasps. "Okay, yes, okay!"

"What movie do you want to watch?" Ferris asks excitedly, jumping onto the bed Jack is on.

"Give the man some space!" Adeel says.

Jack laughs. "Guys, it's not that big of a deal."

"Jack Finch wanting to watch a movie with us at..." Ferris checks their watch and gasps. "8:13 at night?! Unheard of!"

Jack is taken aback. Do they really think he's that boring? He thinks back on all the movies he's watched with them throughout the years and realizes with a sinking feeling he can't recall more than one. And it was a 2 PM matinee.

"Well? What movie, Jack?" Austin asks.

"Whatever you guys want."

"But this is a momentous occasion. We want to make sure we pick something you'll enjoy."

"Honestly, guys," Jack says, laughter in his voice, "whatever you want."

They end up deciding on Ferris's recommendation, *Ghostly Love 2,* the second in a long franchise of ghost-based romance movies. In this particular installment in the riveting saga, Penelope Peters, a Hollywood starlet, falls in love with a ghost on the set of her horror movie.

The team watches as she encounters him for the first time. He's wearing one of the movie-within-the-movie's full-body monster costumes, so Penelope has no idea there's no one but a ghost inside. Penelope flirts with him, and the actress's delivery is way over the top and Jack fights the urge to roll his eyes at every other line.

Ferris gasps when she unmasks her suitor and discovers the monster suit is empty. Penelope screams, startling Adeel, who spills his popcorn.

"Come on," Jack mutters with a smile. Though the movie is insufferable, watching it with his favorite people is actually pretty fun. He laughs at their huge reactions and how immersed they are in the terrible story.

About two thirds through, Jack hears Cecil yawn next to him on the couch, and soon he feels a light pressure on his shoulder. Jack screws his eyes shut, hoping Cecil hasn't fallen asleep on him. He glances over and sees exactly that. Jack finds himself wanting to brush Cecil's curly blond hair out of his sleeping face.

"OMG," Lydia whispers. Jack looks up to see her staring at them, covering her mouth. "OMG!"

Ferris looks over and laughs. "Look at the happy couple," they say, elbowing Austin.

Lydia takes a photo and Jack says, panicked, "No, Lydia, no, delete that."

"Blackmail," she whispers.

"I'm serious, Lydia,"—Cecil stirs on his shoulder and Jack lowers his voice—"please delete that."

Lydia holds up her phone and taunts him with it. Jack grabs at it, but wakes Cecil up in the process.

"Oh, Jack, I'm sorry! Was I sleeping on you?"

"Yeah, but it's okay."

"That is so embarrassing," Cecil says, laughing with his hands on his cheeks.

They go back to watching the movie, Jack hyper aware of how close Cecil is sitting next to him, four of them squeezed into the same small couch.

The movie ends abruptly, trying to set up *Ghostly Love 3*, but Ferris informs them that the first two movies were actually removed from canon and don't matter to the rest of the story.

"Then why did we just sit through that?" Lydia asks.

"Because it's good," Ferris retorts.

Jack glances at his phone: 11:36 PM. That was a long movie. He yawns and stretches his arms forward.

Cecil glances at Jack. "I'm about ready for bed, you guys," he says, subconsciously mimicking Jack's yawn and stretch.

"Me too," Austin agrees, and ushers half the team into the other suite, leaving Jack, Adeel, and Lydia to get ready for bed.

"Lydia, please delete that photo," Jack says once they're alone. "I hate blackmail."

"You'll be fine; just don't do anything to make me post it."

Jack sighs. He hates her. He loves her, but he hates her.

Jack has a good feeling about their next stop. They arrive in the afternoon, the sun beating down at a slant. After a few minutes of struggling, Austin successfully parallel parks in front of the row of townhomes.

"15B," he says, scanning the walls for the right numbers.

"There it is." Austin points to a baby blue townhome with white trim. It has a tiny porch out front with a pair of beaten up work boots on the stoop.

Austin trots up the steps and pushes the buzzer. The door opens and a tall woman in a blue dress appears.

"Hey!" she says excitedly. "Come in, come in!"

The inside of the home is just as cute as the outside, complete with hanging plants, rattan chairs, and a wall perfectly cluttered with photos and paintings.

"I'm Paula. Please, make yourselves at home!"

"Is your husband coming?" Jack asks as he sits down.

The woman frowns at him, confused. "Pardon?"

"Your husband. There were two names on the submission..? Chris?" Jack trails off as he senses that he's gotten himself into trouble.

"Um, yes, my *wife,* Chris, will be down in just a moment." She eyes him curiously, then glances at Cecil and Ferris, the two obviously queer people, clearly questioning why there's such a bigot on the team.

"I apologize, ma'am. I have no problem with you having a wife."

"Well, thank you for your permission," she says coldly.

"Sorry about him," Ferris says.

"No, that's—But the work boots—Homophobic, I am *not.*" Jack takes a breath. "I'm so sorry," he whispers.

"What's goin' on?" A broad-shouldered woman with her hair in a low bun appears at the bottom of the stairs. She puts her hand on Paula's shoulder.

"Nothing, honey."

Paula's wife shakes the team's hands and says, "Hey, guys. I'm Christine."

Adeel and Ferris start filming.

"So what's going on in this lovely home?" Lydia asks.

"Well," Christine says, and the energy shifts. "Paula has been seeing a spirit for quite a while."

"Okay," Lydia says. "What have you been seeing? When and where does it manifest?"

Paula takes a breath and Christine squeezes her hand. "It's a white guy, my height, dark hair." She sighs and adds, "It's actually my ex-husband. He died a few years ago."

"I'm sorry for your loss," Cecil says.

To their surprise, Paula laughs. "Don't be. He was an asshole. We got divorced a few years before. I thought I'd never have to see him again but..."

"So where does he appear?"

Christine answers, "In our bedroom."

Cecil gasps. "Oh no! That's..."

"Awful? Yeah," Christine says.

"So do you both see him?"

"It was only me at first," Paula says, "but Chris started seeing him pretty soon after."

"Did he ever live in this house?" Lydia asks.

"No, never. And he died a hundred miles away."

Lydia looks confused. "Interesting." She moves on, asking, "So what time does he appear?"

The women look at each other. "It's not always a specific time," Paula says carefully.

"Okay..." Lydia says.

"It's when... the two of us..."

Lydia looks confused for a beat, then her jaw drops.

"I don't get it," Cecil says. Ferris whispers in his ear and he gasps and covers his mouth. "Oh no!" His face then changes to one of disgust and he repeats, "Oh no..."

"Yeah. So, you can see why we want him gone."

"Yeah, for sure," Lydia says. "Okay, so we're gonna get all our gear out of the van, and we'll get started."

When the team carries the bags of tech and the table into the house, they see that Paula and Christine have cleared a space in their living room for them.

Ferris gets to work setting up all the gadgets as the couple speaks with Austin.

Jack sits on the pushed-back couch next to Adeel and rests his head in his hands.

"Pretty crazy, huh?" Adeel says. "Ex-husband... That's rough."

"Yeah," Jack says, voice muffled in his hands. He sighs and slumps back on the couch. "They think I'm a homophobe. Me. A homophobe."

"You do kind of have that vibe sometimes."

"What?"

Adeel smiles sympathetically. "It's okay. You're a white man. It happens."

Jack groans. Curse his 99.8% Eastern European genealogy. He looks at Ferris, who is neither white nor a man, and is visibly queer. Ferris never gets mistaken for a homophobe. Why can't Jack be queerer on the outside? Maybe he should try eyeliner.

Cecil walks over and plops down on the couch next to him. "Tough stuff."

Jack nods.

"I can't imagine being them."

Jack nods again.

Cecil looks over. "Hello? Are you back to not speaking to me?"

"What? No," Jack says. "It's not you. I just hate that I have a 'homophobic vibe.'"

Cecil makes a face. "Homophobic vibe? Who told you that?"

Jack gestures to Adeel.

"Oh, hush. You don't have a homophobic vibe at all. How could you? You're queer."

"Well, yeah, but people don't know that just by looking at me."

"If they have an ounce of sense, they do, honey. I clocked you as queer the second I saw you, even through all the glaring and huffing around."

Jack sits up straighter. "Really?"

Cecil smiles at him, amused. "Yeah."

Jack lets out a sigh and relaxes. "Okay, good."

"You think I'd be flirting with you so much if I thought you were straight? Please."

What? Flirting with him? Huh? Jack's brain short circuits and he's about to ask him to clarify when Austin calls Cecil over.

"Oh, sorry, hon. Be back."

Jack stares at him blankly as he walks away.

"You okay, Jack?" Adeel asks.

"Uh-huh," Jack says, not very confident in that answer.

Jack is walking the small upstairs area with a temp reader and EMF meter while Lydia narrates to Adeel's camera.

"Malevolent entities aren't always demons," she says.

"They never are," Jack deadpans.

"Sometimes," she continues, "they're people with negative intentions. The question with this case is how this entity became attached to this location. He didn't die here, he didn't live here, and god knows he isn't welcome here." She pauses and faces the camera. "In order for Cecil to banish this entity, we need to find out what's keeping him here. Let's go check."

With that, Adeel cuts. "You're so good at that, Lydia," he says in awe.

"Years of practice," she says, flipping her hair.

"Maybe one day... I can be in front of the camera," Adeel wonders out loud.

Lydia reaches up and ruffles his hair. "One day, bud."

"Take my place, Adeel," Jack jokes. "Let's switch."

"Really?"

Jack thinks for a moment. "You know what, yeah."

Adeel scrunches his eyebrows. "What?"

"Come here." Jack sets his meters down on the railing beside him. He holds out his hand to takes the camera from Adeel and switches places with him.

"What do I do?" Adeel asks.

"Whatever you want. Talk about the investigation."

"Okay, okay." Adeel takes a deep breath and Jack watches him out of the viewfinder as he centers himself. "Hey guys, it's your boy, Adeel, comin' to you live from—Oh, wait, we're not live. Jack, can we—"

"You guys can edit it out. Keep going."

"Okay. Um, we're here in a haunted location searching for anything out of the ordinary. We haven't found anything yet, but rest assured,"—Adeel comes closer and points a finger at the camera—"if there is anything amiss in this home, we will find it. Mark my words." He steps back and looks at Jack with a huge smile on his face. "How was that?"

"...Maybe a little intense there at the end, but otherwise, perfect." Jack hands the camera back to Adeel and picks up his meters.

Lydia ruffles Adeel's hair again. "Good job, buddy. We ready to join the others?" Lydia asks.

"Uh, one sec," Jack says. Something warm has lit up on his temp reader. Jack squints into the dark master bedroom and moves closer to get a better look. He sees something glinting on the dresser and identifies it as a locket.

"How're you guys doing?" he hears Cecil say as he walks over. "Oh, Jack, what'd you find?" Cecil joins him by the dresser.

"Not sure. It showed up as warm, but she probably just took it off recently or something. It could still be warm from that."

"Or it's the tether."

As the name suggests, a tether is an item, person, or place that keeps an entity rooted to the Earth after they have passed on. It's possible the necklace is the tether, but in a house this full of knick-knacks, it could be any number of things. He figures the locket is as good a place as any to start, though.

Cecil carefully picks up the circular charm and pools the thin chain in his other hand. He looks at Jack. "This is it."

Together they walk back out and down the stairs.

"Find something?" Austin asks curiously.

Ferris trains their camera on Cecil.

"Yeah, Jack spotted this locket and as soon as I picked it up... I can tell. It's this."

"How do you know?" Lydia asks.

"The second I touched it, I felt this... rage. *Very* 'white man.'"

Jack frowns. "You're a white man."

"Yeah, but not like that. This is just full of anger."

"What's inside the locket?" Jack asks.

Cecil pries it open. "Aww. It's a picture of Christine." He turns it toward the camera and Ferris zooms in.

That's puzzling. "Then why is the ex-husband tied to it?"

"Maybe he gave it to her?" Lydia suggests.

"Maybe..." Cecil starts, "but from what I've seen, when consciousnesses are tied to an object, it's usually something very close to their heart. Not usually just some gift. They really have to be invested in it."

"I'll text Paula," Austin says. Only a minute later, he reads her message: "'OMG I should have known it was that locket. He gave it to me a month before we divorced. He said he got it at some flea market and thought of me. I switched out his picture with Christine's, but I guess he could still be attached to it.'"

Cecil doesn't look convinced. "I don't know."

"What, you don't believe her?" Austin asks.

"No, I don't believe *him*. It's not just some locket he found. Like I said, he had to put some serious energy into it. He's so malicious, so negative, and dare I say, *evil*. I think this locket is cursed."

Oh jeez. Jack rolls his eyes. First demons, now curses? What else will he have to debunk for the public?

"Cursed?" Lydia repeats. "You really think so? I mean, like... that's a real thing?"

"Maybe not cursed with a magic spell, but definitely cursed with a terrible intention. I think he knew he was tethering himself and filled this necklace with evil intent. Awful man."

"So what can be done?" Lydia asks. "Can they just throw away the locket?"

Cecil thinks for a moment, then says, "Austin, when do we have to leave for the next stop tomorrow?"

"Uh, probably in the afternoon."

"So we have time for a quick trip tomorrow morning with the homeowners?"

"...Yeah."

"Perfect."

The next morning finds Paula, Christine, and the team standing just beyond a chain link fence. Jack pinches his nose.

Ahead of them sprawls miles and miles of trash.

"The dump," Cecil says. "The perfect final resting place for that piece of garbage."

"You ready babe?" Christine asks Paula, who nods.

She rears back and flings the locket as far into the trash pile as she can. It knocks against a bike tire, an old fridge, and finally comes to rest in a puddle of unidentifiable sludge.

"You took my picture out first, right?" Christine jokes.

Paula elbows her and says, "Of course, silly." They laugh, a weight clearly having been lifted off both their shoulders.

Ferris hangs out the passenger-side window waving at the couple as they stand outside of their home.

"Bye!" Cecil calls out the window.

"Thank you for everything!" they call back.

Cecil sits back in his seat as they drive away.

"Well done, Cecil," Jack says. He can accept his loose definition of 'curse'. He agrees that some people can certainly cast curses just by existing. Jack hopes he has never been that person for anyone. He glances at Cecil and sighs. He remembers how rude he had been to him at the start of the tour. What a white man thing to do. Jack resolves never to be such a negative presence for anyone again. (10 bucks says it doesn't last a day.)

CHAPTER  7

A day? It lasts even less.

After they leave the couple, they head straight to their next stop. Jack wipes his palms on his knees as he realizes their final stop is growing closer and closer: the Amerigo House.

The Amerigo House is an infamous haunted location, and the only well-known location they're visiting on this tour. When Austin realized their route was going to end right by the house, he made sure to include it as their last stop, knowing how much Jack has always wanted to visit.

Jack isn't excited to go just because of the haunting itself, however. Instead, he's eager to debunk the widely-held belief that the home is infested by a demon.

As Jack's dad taught him, all things that exist can be studied and understood, so Jack's default mode is the scientific method. Through all of Jack's research and data, nothing has ever indicated that demons exist. Psychics, either.

When Austin and Jack first connected after college, Austin was endlessly confused by Jack: the skeptical ghost hunter. He couldn't understand how a paranormal researcher could possibly be a skeptic ("You believe in *ghosts,* man!"). Jack does believe in ghosts, but that's just it—for someone to be a successful ghost hunter, they *have* to be a skeptic. Paranormal researchers have to sift through tons of evidence, parsing faux from fact. Jack would insist that all ghost hunters are skeptics. They have to be to make it in this field. (Those who don't fall for demon theories, at least.)

Jack can't believe they're over halfway done with the tour. They're on the sixth stop already.

That means the seventh stop is coming up soon, too. Jack thinks back to Cecil's message from the first house call—accept what is or lose something he loves—and takes a deep breath, hoping he's done enough, accepted Cecil enough, to avoid the consequences.

But why is he listening to a psychic in the first place? Jack may be starting to like Cecil as a person, but he still doubts his credibility as a psychic medium (not that one *can* have credibility as a psychic medium).

He glances over at Cecil who sits happily listening to music in his headphones. Jack sighs. He shouldn't have let him in like he did. Sure, he's funny, and sure, he's Jack's type—blonde with an attitude (though he'd be even better with glasses)—and sure, Jack has begun to kind of enjoy being around him, but he decides it's time to back away. He has a dying aunt, and Cecil's a 'grief vulture'. Not a good combination. Jack looks back out the window.

They arrive at the sixth stop around 2 PM. The house they pull up to looks just as normal as the others. Jack has learned to stop judging the homes by their covers. Apparently, any type of home can be haunted.

It's a small midcentury house with a slanted roof and fifties-style metal awnings. It has flower beds in front of the windows with beautiful red blooms.

Lydia walks up to the matching red door and Ferris starts filming.

Before Lydia even rings the bell, the door swings open and a young girl who looks to be just out of high school opens the door. She's smiling ear to ear and looks at each of them individually.

"Hi!" she says excitedly. "I was looking out the peephole."

"Hi," Lydia says slowly. "Are you Camilla?"

"Yes!" Camilla stands there grinning at them, then jumps out of the doorway and says, "Oh, sorry! Come in!"

"She must be excited for this ghost to be gone," Austin says to Jack.

They follow her into the home and Lydia and Cecil sit on the couch.

Jack goes to sit down next to him, but Camilla exclaims, "Oh my god!"

Jack stands back up, worried he has done something wrong.

"Oh, no, no, you can sit," she clarifies. "I just can't believe the Ghost Checkers are sitting on my couch."

Got it. She's a fan. That explains her odd behavior. No one thus far on the tour has been starstruck by them. Jack prefers the anonymity, but he has been wondering when they'd get to a real fan of theirs. Most of the other clients had just applied through an online form, and likely had never seen an episode of theirs before then.

"So, Camilla," Lydia begins, and Camilla smiles even bigger at the sound of her saying her name. "What exactly have you been seeing?"

"Okay, so, I've been seeing this shadow guy. He walks around at night and almost flickers. I've also been having extremely scary dreams," Camilla says with a smile.

"What kind of dreams?"

"Very Satanic," she replies in the same cheery voice.

"Okay," Lydia says. "So when did the apparitions start?"

"September 24th."

"Wow, you know the date."

"Yes, because that's when the haunted box I ordered arrived."

Come again? "Did you know it was haunted when you bought it?" Jack asks.

"Well, yeah. It was in the title of the listing."

"Where did you get it?" Lydia asks.

"eBay."

"You can buy haunted objects on eBay?" Cecil asks.

"Yeah," Camilla answers. "They're all over. Dolls, mirrors, rings. And even mystery boxes, like I got."

"Mystery box?"

"Yeah. It's a box you buy online but you don't know what's in it until you open it. This one was a haunted one."

"So what was in it?"

Camilla squints, looking up and to the right, then lists as she counts on her fingers, "A half-burned candle, a corn husk doll, a couple teeth... oh, and a jar of ashes."

"Can we see the box?" Jack asks.

"Sure! I keep it by my bed." Camilla goes to grab it.

Cecil knocks his knee against Jack's and says, "This is pretty ridiculous, huh?"

Jack glances at him. *Keep your distance.* "Mm-hm."

Camilla comes back with a small cardboard box, contents jostling around as she walks. She sets it on the coffee table and the team leans forward to get a better look.

She wasn't lying. The box contains exactly what she said.

Lydia reaches in and carefully picks up the jar. It's a spice jar with the label torn off, and in marker, it says 'Human Remains'. "Can you legally ship this?" she wonders.

Cecil takes it from her and cocks his head. He glances around at his teammates and Camilla before taking the lid off. He sniffs it briefly.

"What are you—" Jack starts.

Before Jack can get the words out, Cecil dips his finger in and takes a taste.

"What the *fuck?*" Ferris says from behind the camera.

Cecil laughs and hands the open jar to Lydia who looks horrified. She takes it slowly, in shock.

"Smell," he instructs her. She stares at him, searching his eyes before lowering her nose close to the top of the jar and taking a whiff.

She sneezes.

"See?" Cecil says. "It's black pepper."

Camilla looks surprised. "What? But it says human remains."

Cecil looks at the other items in the box. "Yeah... I think you got scammed, Cam."

Camilla frowns. "Darn." She thinks for a moment, then says, "Wait, then what about the shadow guy?"

"Now *he* could be real. We'll have to..." Cecil looks directly into Ferris's camera and they zoom in, "check and see."

The team stands, and Ferris finishes setting up the tech table. Jack watches as Lydia and Adeel sidle up to Camilla and start talking. He can't quite hear what they're saying, but he sees Lydia put Adeel's arm around herself, and Camilla seems to notice. Jack rolls his eyes when he realizes they're still just playing their little scandal game.

After Camilla leaves for the next few hours, the team begins their walkthrough.

"So how'd you know it was pepper before you tasted it? Super lucky guess?" Ferris asks Cecil.

"Well, when I picked it up, there was just... nothing. When I pick up an old scarf, I know someone's whole life story. Picking up their literal ashes and feeling nothing at all? Nuh-uh."

"That makes sense," Lydia says.

If it were Jack, he wouldn't trust such a lucky guess. Cecil must really believe in himself.

Jack and Adeel walk into one of the bedrooms and Jack holds his EMF meter out in front of him. He frowns as its lights flicker between red and green over and over. "Weird," he mutters, and smacks it against his other palm. Jack turns and sees Cecil standing in the doorway.

"Anything?" Cecil asks.

Jack shakes his head. "No. You?"

"Nothing." Cecil pans his flashlight around the room. Adeel walks out to film B-roll. Jack and Cecil stand quietly before Cecil says, "So... Camilla's somethin' else, huh?"

"*Right?*"

They let out stifled laughs.

"I mean— she bought"—Cecil interrupts himself with laughter and grabs Jack's shoulder—"a mystery box online..."

"Full of garbage," Jack adds.

"Full of garbage!" Cecil repeats. He snorts and brings a hand to his nose. "Black pepper, Jack! It was honest-to-god just out of someone's spice cabinet, I swear."

"Mystery boxes seem like a lucrative business. Just put junk... in a box."

"It could literally be anything, too," Cecil adds. "Old baby teeth? In the box."

Despite himself, Jack cracks a smile.

"Creepy doll made of garbage?"

"In the box," Jack says.

"A candle you already burned half of?"

"Put it in the box."

Cecil grabs Jack's shoulder again as he lets out high-pitched, hiccupping laughs. He sighs as his laughter dissipates. "Oh, lord."

Jack lets his smile drop and he chews his cheek. He shrugs his shoulder so Cecil lets go of him. *Shit.* He doesn't want to like him so much. Jack can't let himself forget that while Cecil might be fun to talk to, he's still lying to Jack's friends. Jack almost lost sight of that. "Hey, you know where Lydia is?" Jack asks.

"Kitchen."

Jack and Cecil walk back down the short hallway and find the kitchen, where Lydia is standing with her own EMF meter out.

She turns around and says, "Guys, what the hell?" She shows them her meter, which is lighting up randomly just like Jack's. So it's not just his. Weird.

"What does that mean?" Cecil asks.

"Means something's up," Lydia answers cryptically, and Jack can tell it's for the camera. "Ferris, what are your sensors doing?"

"EMF is going crazy, and the EVP won't even turn on," they call from the living room a short distance away.

"Does that mean there's a presence?" Cecil asks.

"Not necessarily, but something's definitely messing with the frequencies," Lydia answers, holding her EMF meter above her head as if trying to find bars for a cell phone.

"God, all my tech is going crazy. Adeel, how's your camera?" Ferris asks.

"It seems okay."

"Austin, what do you want us to do?"

"Investigate. Something's obviously going on here. Cecil, feel anything?"

"Not yet."

"Lydia, walk with Cecil through the house and see if any energy spikes correspond with how he feels," Austin instructs. "Adeel, go with them. Ferris, you and Jack continue your walkthrough."

Ferris grabs his camera rig and follows Jack.

"Pretty cool how they're using tech *and* Cecil's ability together, don't ya think?" Ferris says as they walk around a room Jack's already been through twice.

"Yeah, I don't know." Jack pauses, then asks, "Uh... is the mic on?"

Ferris groans. "No, literally nothing is working right. Something's seriously messing with all the electronics."

In that case... "Well, okay, no. I don't believe in Cecil *at all.*" Jack stops walking and faces Ferris, who lowers his camera. "He's a nice guy, and he was right about the black pepper, *thank god,* but this whole psychic act isn't fooling me. Psychics aren't real. They aren't. It's just a fact."

"I thought you guys were becoming friends."

Jack laughs. "No matter how nice he is, and no matter what the public thinks of us, he claims he's a psychic. We'll never be friends."

"Got something," Lydia calls from the living room.

Ferris and Jack join the rest of the team, currently crowded around the cardboard box.

"Cecil, tell them," Lydia encourages.

"Okay, well, the pepper obviously wasn't anything, but I realized I didn't touch the other items. These teeth are definitely something."

"The teeth? Can they even hold enough energy to affect our electronics like this?" Austin asks.

"Maybe that's exactly why they're affecting them the way they are," Ferris chimes in. "So spotty and intermittent. My mic was turning itself on and off every few seconds."

"So what do we do?" Lydia asks.

"If it really is the teeth," Jack starts, "we should encase them in salt."

"On it." Lydia goes to the kitchen and comes back with a bowl of kosher salt. She picks up the teeth and places them in the bowl, moving the salt to cover them. "Now what?"

"They should probably stay in there for a day or so. If she wants to keep them, she can take them out after that, or just throw them away, but somewhere not near the house."

Austin calls Camilla and lets her know she can come back. When she arrives, they update her on what they found.

"Thank god it's easy to get rid of it, huh? I mean, I bought the box hoping to get on your show but I guess I didn't think about how an actual ghost would be in my house."

Wait a minute. "You what?" Jack asks.

Camilla stays quiet for a moment. "Uh…"

"You're telling me…" Lydia begins, "that you knowingly brought a ghost into your home to lure us here?"

"Well, when you put it like that it sounds bad, but guys, I'm probably your biggest fan—"

"Yeah, I'd say so," Ferris says. "Haunt your own house so we'd show up? You're the only person in the world who'd do that."

Jack and Austin exchange a look. They'll discuss that later.

"Guys, come on—"

"We appreciate how much you love the show," Austin begins diplomatically, "but Camilla, buddy, you could have brought in an entity that was way more intense, even malevolent. You've gotta be careful with this stuff."

"It's not a game," Jack says.

"I know that. I'm sorry," Camilla says, eyes downcast.

Cecil pats her on the shoulder. "Well, thankfully, it was an easy fix, so no harm done."

Jack agrees. He's glad nothing went wrong on this stop of the tour. Something easily could have.

CHAPTER 18

"Jack," Cecil whines from the pullout couch, "it happened again."

"More rumors?" Jack asks.

"Yes," Cecil says, stress pulling his voice tight. Cecil hands Jack his phone and covers his face. "I don't know what to do."

Jack reads the tweet Cecil has pulled up on the screen: *it's like they're doing this to us on purpose I LITERALLY CAN'T*. He watches the attached video. It's a zoomed in clip of one of the TikToks the rest of the team made back at the museum. In the background, Cecil and Jack are perusing the third-floor exhibits and even Jack can see that they look like they're very much enjoying each other's company. His cheek finds its way between his teeth. Interesting.

There is a reply under it from @camillaluvslydia: '*no but for real, they were at my house yesterday and there was so much chemistry between them i was DYING*'.

Cecil holds his hand out to take his phone back, but Jack scrolls up and keeps watching the clip as it plays over and over. Video-Jack's eyes are as soft as his smile as he listens to Cecil talk. He definitely needs to get that in check.

Jack hands the phone back to Cecil and says to Austin, "Please be mindful of what is in the background of your videos. It is causing problems."

Austin looks over the rim of his glasses from the small desk in the hotel room. "Maybe you should be mindful of what you're doing in the background of our videos," he shoots back and pushes his glasses up by the middle.

"Guys, guys," Lydia says, "maybe we should all be mindful of making sure *Adeel and I* are in the background of our videos."

"What?" Austin asks, confused.

"Yeah, Lydia and I are publicly pretending to secretly date because Jack and Cecil don't appreciate their fame," Adeel explains, sounding very rehearsed.

Austin nods slowly.

"So maybe just make sure to get incriminating footage of us in the background, okay?" Lydia says.

"Uh-huh, uh-huh... No," Austin says.

"Well, wouldn't both of these scandals increase views, though?" Ferris points out. "So isn't all of this kind of good?"

"It's never good to have lies spread on the internet," Cecil says, like a PSA about online safety.

"These people," Lydia says quietly to Adeel, who shakes his head.

"Okay, well, we have actual rumors right now," Cecil says, "so we need to focus on making sure those go away."

"We could have a livestream?" Ferris suggests.

Immediately, Jack and Cecil object because historically, livestreams have not been on their side, but Ferris cuts them off.

"A livestream where you can actually talk to the fans and address the rumors instead of hoping they just disappear. They never just disappear," Ferris adds, obviously referring to how the fans had latched onto 'Lerris' and even now, haven't stopped tweeting Lydia and Ferris fanart of them.

"That's... actually a good idea," Jack agrees.

"I'm full of 'em," they reply, pretending to flip their short hair.

"Okay, so livestream in the morning?" Austin asks.

"I'm in," Cecil says. "How about you, Jack?"

"Yep," Jack sighs. When will the nightmare end?

The next morning the team meets in the hallway and walks down to breakfast together. Lydia and Adeel are talking excitedly to each other about ways to slip their 'relationship' into the livestream.

"Okay, okay, so you put your arm around my shoulders, I'll whisper a joke to you, and you laugh really hard. Does that sound okay?" she asks him.

Adeel scratches his cheek, thinking. "I just wonder if it's enough?"

"No, that's definitely enough," Ferris says sarcastically, plopping their plate down on the table and taking a seat.

Cecil is standing at the waffle iron when Jack walks over to get a banana. He notices he's frowning a little more than someone normally would when making a waffle.

"All good?" Jack asks.

"Well—" Cecil starts, crossing his arms. "I don't understand how it's supposed to start?"

"You turn it over."

"What?"

"Like this." Jack grabs the handle and rotates the waffle iron, starting the countdown.

"What in god's name..."

"Haven't you ever made a hotel waffle before? I think they're all like that."

"I was branching out," Cecil says with a shrug. "That's what I get for trying new things."

Jack chuckles and walks back to the table, Cecil following a minute or so later.

"Hey, hey," Austin greets them. "We were just talking about the livestream later. You guys looking forward to it?"

"Yep!" Cecil answers brightly. "Be good to finally get these fans to simmer down, huh?" he says to Jack, who nods.

Jack looks down at his plate and pushes a little sausage lump around in his gravy. He glances over at Cecil who happily munches away at his waffle. "Yeah. I'm not a fan of this internet stuff."

"Well you better learn to fake it, and *fast*," Lydia says, "because we're going live at 11 EST, baby!"

"You've been calling people 'baby' a lot," Ferris comments.

"Yeah."

"You should stop that."

"Alright, babe."

"Worse," Ferris says. "So much worse."

A few minutes before 11 finds the team hanging out in one hotel room yet again. Before Jack can mentally prepare, it's time to stream.

Cecil and Jack sit together on the edge of the bed facing Lydia's phone, which is propped against the TV. The rest of the team crowds in behind them.

Lydia hits the button to go live and climbs up on the bed, too.

"Good morning, y'all!" Cecil says.

Jack feels his heart in his throat. He hates live public speaking, and even more when it's personal, but Cecil has no problem speaking.

"We are coming to you live for the purpose of dispelling some rumors going around about us. We have been seeing lots of tweets regarding Jack and I's relationship." Cecil grabs Jack's hand, then quickly lets it go when he realizes it's not helping their case. "To all of you spreading those rumors and overanalyzing footage: Stop it! You're doing more harm than good," he says in a playful tone, but it's clear he means it.

"Uh-huh," Jack says, then remembers how Adeel told him not to say anything if he doesn't have anything to add, so he adds, "We're not together. I don't even like him."

Cecil laughs brightly. "Okay, right."

Jack turns to him and says quietly, "What?"

Cecil replies at the same volume, "...What, you're serious? We're friends. Of course you like me."

"Well, yeah, we're friends, but I don't—Okay, what I'm trying to say is—"

"Oh my god, save me from the awkwardness!" Ferris cries.

"They're not together guys, bye!" Lydia leans forward on all fours to reach for her phone but loses her balance and knocks into Jack, who knocks forward into Cecil.

With his mouth.

It's quick, and Jack's sure no one even saw. It probably looked like they just bumped. It didn't look like a kiss. It didn't.

But then Jack looks over at the chat, and judging by all the comments in all caps, it must have.

"Kiss?!" Lydia exclaims nonsensically, sitting back up.

Adeel must take this as an instruction, because he grabs her and they crash together into a kiss.

"Okay, bye!" Austin says as he ends the livestream.

Lydia and Adeel separate and Adeel says, "Did it work?"

"What was the intended result?" Ferris asks incredulously.

Adeel looks at them blankly.

Jack turns to Cecil. His eyes are wide and he's staring at Jack with his hand lightly covering his mouth.

Jack chews on his cheek, then tastes peach chapstick that he wasn't wearing.

"That went pretty well, I think," Adeel says.

"What livestream were *you* at?" Lydia asks.

Jack feels a buzz in his pocket. It's Mel. "I'll be back, guys." He stands from the bed and steps out of the room before answering. "So you just saw that?"

"Oh, my dear boy, I just saw that."

Jack huffs out a laugh. "I just can't win, Mel."

"Oh, please. You kiss a cute little celebrity on the mouth and you say you can't win."

"I didn't want to, though. I didn't mean to."

"It's fate, Jackie! It's—oh, hold on." Her voice gets quieter as she speaks to someone else. "No, I don't—he doesn't need to—"

The phone clatters as someone takes it from her. A deeper voice takes over, saying, "Hello, son. Mel doesn't want you to know this, but she's in the hospital."

In the background, Mel says, "No, I'm not!"

"Yes, she is."

"What happened?" Jack asks.

"She accidentally let me know that her dizziness had not abated since her last visit to urgent care."

"It's not a big deal," Mel says in the background.

"Is she okay?" Jack asks.

"Yes, she's fine. Difficult, but fine."

"Hey!" Mel says.

"Can I talk to her again?"

"Of course." Jack's father hands the phone back to Mel.

"I'm sorry about him, Jackie."

"You weren't gonna tell me you're still sick? You—you weren't gonna tell anyone?"

"Jack—"

"You're really important to me. I don't want anything to happen to you."

"I know, sweet boy." Mel pauses. "I'm sorry."

"It's okay. Just, please be honest, okay? I love you."

"I love you, too, sweetpea."

Jack asks her about how she's feeling and they chat a while more before they hang up. Jack leans back against the wall of the hallway. Why would she lie about this? Why would she be so flippant about her health? Doesn't she know how important she is?

Jack sighs. She's always been this way. Why would she change?

He heads back into the hotel room and the team looks worried at the sight of his expression.

"What's up?" Austin asks.

"Mel's sick again. Or—still is. Has been. She was lying to everyone."

"That's awful Jack, I'm sorry," Austin says.

"Is there anything we can do?" Ferris asks, reaching a hand out for him.

Jack smiles and squeezes it, but shakes his head.

"Oh, we were just talking about where to go to lunch. Do you wanna pick?" Lydia says.

"No, that's okay. I think I'm just gonna hang out here. You guys go."

The team looks hesitant to leave him, but Jack says, "Today has just been a lot. I just want some space, I think. You guys go."

They each hug him, then set out for some kind of Mexican frog-themed restaurant.

The door unlocks with a click a few hours later and Jack blinks awake. His book is open on his lap and the last thing he remembers is rereading the same paragraph four times, but he still has no idea what it was about. He closes his book and lays it to the side as the team files in.

Their presence is a stark difference from their absence. Jack can appreciate being alone. He has always preferred quiet to noise. Some people even turn on recordings of coffee shop ambience because they can't stand to be alone in silence, but Jack actually enjoys it.

The sound of the team's presence is different. Jack savors the sound of Austin's attempts at corralling the others, Lydia and Ferris's wisecracks, Adeel's nervous voice. Even Cecil's laugh this past week or so.

Just then, Cecil walks into the bedroom of the suite with a white Styrofoam box.

"Got this for you," Cecil says, holding it out to Jack.

He takes it and is surprised by the weight. He opens it to find a heaping mound of fried pickles. Jack looks up at Cecil, who stands awkwardly.

"I can put them on the counter if you don't want them," Cecil says, reaching to take the box from Jack, but he stops him.

"How'd you know?"

"Know..?"

"That these are my favorite?"

"Oh," Cecil says, and looks proud. "Your grandma told me."

Psychics may not be real, but Cecil's definitely a good guesser, because fried pickles have been his favorite snack since he was seven. His grandma used to fix them for him just the way he liked, even with honey mustard on the side, which she always said was odd. Jack opens the lid of the sauce container to find exactly that.

"How on earth did you know to get honey mustard? I know it's a pretty weird pairing."

Cecil taps his temple and says, "Psychic, remember? Oh, but you hate psychics. I guess I'll just take this back, then," he teases and moves to take the box.

"No way," Jack says. "Touch it and you lose a hand."

"That really *is* your favorite, huh?"

"Best food in the world."

Cecil laughs and sits on the bed.

"Try some," Jack says, picking up a pickle slice and dipping it in the honey mustard. He holds it out to Cecil who takes it, eyeing him with uncertainty before popping it into his mouth.

"Oh my *god*," Cecil says. "That is good. What the hell? Why have I never had these?"

"What's good?" Lydia says leaning into the room as if summoned. "Ooh, what are we eating?" She steps fully into the room and rubs her hands together.

"No," Jack says. "Out."

Lydia looks offended and says, "How come only Cecil gets some?"

"Because Cecil is a guest," Cecil says in the third person. "That was so good," he says to Jack, reaching into the box and taking another.

Jack digs in. Cecil tells him about some zany waiter they had and Jack listens happily. Jack catches himself studying the curve of Cecil's nose and the way he smiles as he speaks. After Cecil's story, Jack says, "Seriously, thank you, Cecil." He wipes his mouth on his hand. "This stuff with my aunt," he begins. "It really gets to me sometimes. She's the strongest woman I've ever met—"

Lydia says, "Hey!" from the other room.

"—and I know she'll be fine, but... I just can't help but wonder, every time this happens... What if she's not?"

Cecil nods and stays quiet for a moment before saying, "What scares you the most about it?"

Jack wants to say 'losing her', but stops. Of course losing her would devastate him, but he's not sure it scares him. He supposes what scares him most is the uncertainty. He has no idea where she would go. Would she become another one of those entities that just drifts for centuries?

Jack voices this, and Cecil replies, "I know you think I'm just a fraud, but in case it's worth anything, I've spoken to a lot of people that have passed on. Not their ghosts, but their energies, their true essences. And not one of them has been unhappy." Cecil pats Jack's leg and stands up. "She'll be okay. Promise."

Jack bites his cheek until it bleeds. *She'll be okay,* he repeats to himself, but can't quite convince himself to believe it. Jack has no idea what a person goes through after they die, only that sometimes they end up tethered to a home or an item or a person. Jack thinks back to the haunted doll from a few houses ago. Cecil himself said that entity was in anguish. Jack can't help but imagine Mel in its place. Cecil said no *essences* have been unhappy, and he knows the residue in the doll wasn't her essence, but still. It could happen, and there's nothing Jack can do about it. No amount of research or measuring or data can help him understand what will happen to his aunt. Jack winces when he bites his cheek again, forgetting it's sore.

Jack takes out his phone and types the message: *'Hey :) Hope you're feeling better. Love you!'* and hits send.

She'll be okay, he thinks. Cecil promised, after all.

CHAPTER 9

Several hours have passed, and Jack has given up on his book. This hotel is not a suite, so Ferris and Adeel are playing Mario Kart at full volume only feet away from where Jack sits trying and failing to focus on reading. Once again, he has read the same paragraph multiple times without realizing, nor comprehending.

He sighs and tosses the book aside and looks over at the rest of the team. Ferris and Adeel sit on the edge of the first bed enraptured in their game. Ferris's feet don't touch the ground, even in their platform boots. Adeel sits with his legs crossed beneath him, a bowl of popcorn balanced on his lap. Lydia is lounging behind them, watching the screen too. She took her shoes off before getting on the bed, and Jack notices her mismatched socks, though both depict dogs. Austin sits looking at his laptop at the small desk, one hand in his hair, the other propping up his chin as he reads what's on the screen.

"I can't believe no one even cared we made out, Adeel," she says, referring to their kiss during the livestream. They had watched their mentions on Twitter and set Google alerts, but no one seems to have noticed or cared about their fake romance.

"Yeah," Adeel says distractedly. "Dammit!" He throws his arms up in the air as the scoreboard displays on the screen, Ferris having won again. Adeel turns to Lydia and says, "Yeah, that's weird. We full-on kissed. Somebody had to have seen."

"We were pretty obvious back there. Maybe Camilla will come through for us," Lydia says.

"She's our biggest fan. Maybe she will," Adeel says.

Austin laughs. "She is not our biggest fan."

"What do you mean?" Adeel asks.

"Jack knows. Remember our meet and greet in Atlanta in 2016?"

"Yes." Jack says.

"Remember the girl with the sign?"

"How could I forget," Jack says flatly. At their first meet and greet after getting pretty big on YouTube, where most of the fans were casual and just wanted to say hello, there was one girl who wanted... a bit more than that. She showed up with a sign that said 'Future Mrs. Finch' and begged both of them to sign her forehead, among other things. "Caty."

"Caty!" Austin laughs. "She liked you," he teases.

Jack groans. He had hoped never to have to think about that girl again. She terrorized him online for months until he stopped reading comments altogether. That was definitely a good choice. They had started to get pretty graphic.

"Jack had a groupie?" Cecil asks, grinning.

"She was not a groupie."

"Jack had a groupie!" Ferris says triumphantly.

"How have I not heard about this girl?" Lydia asks.

"You probably have, actually. Ever see tweets or messages from @jackiesgirl93?"

"Yes, she just called me beautiful in the last Instagram post."

"That's one of her many accounts."

"Really? Huh. Well she has good taste apparently," she says, flipping her hair.

"She liked Jack too," Ferris points out. "I don't know about 'good taste.'" They grin and wink at Jack.

"Hey!" Cecil says. "That's so mean. Jack is a fine-lookin' fella."

Hm. Does he mean 'fine' or 'fiiine'? His southern drawl made it hard to tell. That will torture Jack for eternity.

Wait, no it won't. Jack doesn't care.

"I'm hungry," Ferris whines, falling backwards onto the bed. They reach their arms out to grab at Lydia who smacks them.

"You just had lunch a few hours ago," Jack says.

"Exactly, a few hours ago."

"I can go pick up food?" Cecil offers.

"That'd be great. I'm getting kind of hungry too. Where do we want?" Austin asks.

The team decides on sushi from a nearby sushi bar. Cecil calls in their order, and upon hearing just how many rolls this team can devour, Austin suggests he take someone with him.

"Jack, you wanna go? I have some work to do with Ferris and Adeel."

"What about Lydia?"

"No," she says immediately.

Fine. Jack gets up and slips his sneakers back on and they head out the door after Austin tosses them his keychain (which is not nearly as bulky as Lydia's).

When they get out to the van, Jack holds his hand out for the keys, and looks over when Cecil doesn't give them to him.

"I'm driving," Cecil says.

Jack doesn't know why he thought Cecil couldn't drive. He just has that vibe. Something about the eternal gleam in his eyes makes him look like he doesn't have enough grit to parallel park during a driving test. Jack gets into the passenger seat and they set off.

Maybe Jack was right in saying Cecil can't drive, though. Cecil is a very... careful driver. He has to crank the seat way up to see over the wheel properly, and hunches over it like an old person. He drives the exact speed limit, so they arrive at the restaurant far later than they would have if Jack had driven, but he keeps his mouth shut.

It ends up working out well because their food is ready exactly when they walk in.

"See? Psychic." Cecil taps his temple.

Jack laughs. "Right."

Cecil scoffs. "You *still* don't respect me?"

"No, I respect you fine. I just don't think *this* is a product of psychicness."

"But you do believe me now? That I'm psychic?"

Jack pauses. He has two options here. One: he could be honest and say that, no, he still knows Cecil's a fraud, which would cause tension and confrontation. Or, two: he could tell him what he wants to hear and get back to the hotel for a wonderful evening of sushi. He prefers the latter. "Yeah. You've proven yourself." Jack hates lying, but not as much as he likes sushi.

They arrive back at the hotel after a gruelingly slow drive, and the team decides to watch another movie while they eat.

"*Ghostly Love 6!*" Ferris votes.

"Six? How many are there?" Jack asks.

"Well, there are seven in the main series, but in the same universe, there's a second series called *Haunted Love*. It's totally different. The ghost falls in love first in those ones," they explain.

"How about we let Adeel choose?" Lydia suggests.

"That's a great idea," Austin agrees. "Adeel, what do you want to watch?"

He shifts on the bed nervously. "Well, uh... We could watch my very favorite... I used to watch it when I was at home sick from school, so it's very comforting to me."

"Let's do it," Austin says, handing him the remote.

From what Jack knows about Adeel, he expected a superhero movie, or a buddy comedy, or perhaps even a romcom, but he is sorely mistaken. Adeel chose *Slasher Man 4: Oh No, He's Back*, which is just 104 minutes of brutal murder and gore. Jack has never been so on edge during a movie.

He glances over at Adeel halfway through and is shocked to see a mild, content smile on his face. He really finds this comforting? Jack thinks back on every time he's slept in the same room with this man and shudders.

The movie finally ends when the leading lady gets Slasher-Manned, and the credits roll. Jack doesn't finish his sashimi.

"That was..." Lydia begins.

"...a movie," Ferris finishes.

"Wasn't it?" Adeel agrees with a smile.

"Most definitely," Austin says, side eyeing Adeel.

"Well, Adeel, you have very unique taste. And that's never a bad thing," Cecil adds.

"What'd you think, Jack?" Adeel asks him.

What to say... "I think it was..." He chews his cheek. Jack lied enough earlier today. "Well, it was a bit flawed."

"What?"

"I mean... Okay, how about this—Why was she covered in blood in one scene, and then clean in the next?"

"Maybe she had a wipe?" Adeel suggests.

"Well, even aside from the continuity errors, there's no context for why the killer is killing. What's motivating him? That's something we need to know if we're going to care about a story."

"I don't know," Adeel says, looking down. "I guess it's not a good movie."

Oh no. Are those... tears?

"No, bud, it's a great movie!" Austin says, glaring at Jack.

"I think you made a good choice," Lydia says, patting him on his back.

"It's fine you guys. You know, I'm gonna just go to bed a little early." Adeel gets a key to the second room from Austin and lugs his bag out of the hotel room.

As soon as the door closes, the floodgates open.

"Dude, what the hell?"

"Why would you say that?"

"You *know* he's sensitive!"

"Guys," Jack starts, "I know, I'm sorry. I just hate giving false feedback."

"So just don't say anything," Lydia says, crossing her arms.

"He asked me directly."

"So lie!"

"I don't—" *lie*, he wants to say, but that isn't true anymore. Jack glances at Cecil. "I'm sorry, guys."

"Eh, I'm sure he'll be fine," Lydia says, standing from her place on the bed. "I'll go check on him." She walks out of the room.

"So you really don't lie?" Cecil asks with a smile.

"No." *Lie.*

"So you really believe I'm psychic."

Jack forces a smile. "Yes." *Another lie.* And he thought he was out of untruths for the evening.

What is happening to him? He used to be so firm in his values and morals, and now he's just lying left and right. At least they're rather harmless, as far as lies go.

Cecil hums happily and opens his phone, immersing himself in Twitter.

Jack looks up and sees Austin eyeing him curiously. Austin pulls out his phone and Jack feels his own buzz a moment later.

Austin
?????

> **Jack**
> What

Austin
So do you really think he's psychic????

> **Jack**
> No
> White lie
> No big deal

Austin
And yet u couldn't lie to adeel.......

> Jack leaves him on read.

Lydia and Adeel come back into the room a while later. Adeel looks to be in much higher spirits.

"We have news..." Lydia says. Jack notices they're holding hands. *No...*

"We..." *Please don't say 'Got engaged'.* "...made a Twitter!"

This clearly doesn't get the reaction they were expecting.

"Guys, a fake anonymous Twitter! To tweet rumors about ourselves."

"Oh...kay..." Austin says.

"We messaged @jackiegirl93 that this fake person 'saw' that the two of us are together, so hopefully Caty will spread it."

"You talked to Caty? You actually, voluntarily made contact with her?" Austin asks, shocked.

"Yeah, why?"

"She's crazy! Jack knows."

Jack nods. "Crazy. I wouldn't get mixed up with her if I were you."

"I'm sure it'll be fine."

Later, Lydia is showing Austin their fake Twitter.

"Oh, okay. And the goal is...?"

"To expose our romance."

Austin makes a face. "Are you... together?"

"Pfft, what?" Adeel scoffs. "No way."

"No, this is purely for publicity," Lydia says.

"And you really think this will be that big of a scandal? Haven't you already, like, made out on stream? If it didn't blow up after that, what makes you think Twitter rumors are gonna be more scandalous?"

Lydia and Adeel look blankly at each other. They abandon Austin.

"Jack," Lydia says. "Let me show you our Twitter."

"No," he says once again, trying again to focus on his book.

"Yes." Lydia hops onto his bed and shoves her phone in his face.

The page really does look like a fan's page. The name they put is 'bianca the ghost' with a ghost emoji. The bio is believable too, saying Bianca is a student, cat lover, plant mom, and Ghost Checkers fan. Apparently Bianca also met Ferris in 2018, and proudly displays this in her bio. If Jack saw this profile online, he would believe it was a real page.

It already has 48 followers, so Jack taps the number to see the list. At the top is @jackiesgirl93. Jack hands the phone back, saying, "I thought I told you not to get mixed up with Caty. Block her."

"No, she's a valuable asset to the cause," Adeel says.

Jack rolls his eyes. It's their funeral. He turns back to his book and reads for an hour or so more. It's about a scientist falling in love with an alien she's supposed to dissect. At this point in the story, she can't understand why the alien is so standoffish and cold. Jack wishes he could tell her it's because, to the alien, she's always going to be a threat simply because of the way their relationship began. They wouldn't have had the chance to fall in love in the first place if she hadn't intended to kill him. Their love will always be a result of the threat she posed.

Jack's stomach fills with lead again. That's enough reading for now. Jack puts the book aside and looks at what his teammates are doing.

Lydia, Adeel, and Ferris are watching videos on Lydia's phone, Austin is lounging on the second bed, and Cecil looks to be doodling at the desk.

"What are you doing?" Jack asks.

"I'm checking in with my guides," Cecil answers.

"What are guides?"

"Entities that are attached to you and guide you through life. They can be animal spirits, ancestors, or even never have been on Earth at all."

"So... what most would call demons?"

"Come again?"

"A lot of people think that entities that were never human are demons," Jack explains.

"Oh, for sure no. Some entities just... exist. Nothing more to it." Cecil smiles and Jack smiles back. Good to know he's logical about *something*.

"So what are they telling you? Your guides."

"They're telling me not to trust everything right now. It's apparently going to be difficult to know what's real."

Jack purses his lips. "Weird."

"Really weird, right? I guess maybe we'll have a fake haunting next? Who knows! We'll just have to wait and see, I suppose."

"Guess so." Jack smiles tightly and returns to his book.

CHAPTER 10

The next morning, Jack stares in the mirror, his hair still dripping onto his forehead from the water he splashed on his face. His eyes look tired, distraught, betrayed. His heart pounds with a quiet rage.

How could he do this? How could Austin do this? After years of friendship, years of brotherhood...

He booked a meet and greet behind Jack's back.

Jack hates them. He likes meeting people in small groups where he can keep track of the conversation, but meeting hundreds of people all at once, one after the other, and posing for pictures... That's Jack's personal hell.

Austin knows this, and that's exactly why he didn't tell Jack about the meet and greet until the morning of. Jack can admit, blindsiding him really is the only way to get him there, but Jack doesn't have to like it.

"Ready to go?" Austin asks, looking slick in an off-white button up, red bow tie, and olive-green suspenders. He steps into the bathroom and fixes his hair in the mirror.

"No," Jack replies.

Austin throws an arm around him and looks at him in the mirror. "It's gonna be great, buddy. You always kill at these things."

"No, I don't." Jack is awkward, rude, and unlikeable. He knows this. Hardly any of the show's fans like him.

"Come on, bud. We're leaving in a few."

Jack steps out into the rest of the hotel room. Lydia is wearing a black turtleneck under a black leather jacket with a wallet chain she must have borrowed from Ferris. Ferris is wearing their signature platform boots and an oversized graphic tee layered over a black long sleeve tee. A golden glasses chain glints around their neck. Adeel is wearing a loose and flowy, pink, short-sleeved button up with black skinny jeans.

Jack glances at Cecil and does a double take. He has on a white short-sleeved button up with brown vertical stripes tucked into matching brown slacks. He's leaning over digging in his suitcase and Jack quickly looks away, but not quickly enough to avoid noticing how well Cecil's pants fit. He lifts a cool hand to his face to combat the warmth suddenly rushing to his cheeks.

Jack himself went the more comfortable route while still trying to look at least semi-professional. He's wearing a button up tucked into his jeans with a cardigan over top. These events are always too cold.

"Ready everybody?" Austin asks. The team gathers by the door and they head downstairs to the conference room Austin booked for the meet and greet.

Jack notices several things. The room is set up with a backdrop for the team to stand in front of for pictures. It has their Ghost Checkers logo dotted around the black background. A table next to the backdrop holds some of their merch. Lots of poles with retractable belts are spaced out to form a winding line. It looks very professional, and Jack is once again impressed by Austin's coordination skills.

The main thing Jack notices is that the winding line is completely full.

Hundreds of people, mainly older teen girls, stand excitedly waiting for them, and scream as soon as they walk through the door. Many of the fans are wearing homemade merch shirts, some have handmade signs, and all are cheering for them. A few members of hotel staff help manage the crowd, and the meet and greet gets started.

The first group of fans comprises two young teens and their parents.

"Hi," the mom says with a smile.

"Hey there, folks!" Lydia says.

The two teens flock to her. "You look so pretty!" one of them says.

"Can we get a picture?" the other asks.

"That's what we're here for!" Lydia replies.

They stand against the backdrop. Jack stands on one end with Adeel on the other, and Ferris, Lydia, the fans, and Austin stand in between them. They all smile and their parents take a few pictures before thanking them and moving on.

Jack sighs and pulls his cardigan tighter around himself. It's pretty cold in the big, open room, but he really just wants comfort.

Jack remembers when Austin gave him this cardigan. They were at one of their first meet and greets back in 2016. It wasn't their first, so Jack knew what to expect, but he knew he didn't want to go.

Austin had to coax him out of the hotel room with promises of fried pickles later in the day. He succeeded in getting Jack to the park the meet and greet was taking place at, but it was plain to see Jack was out of his element, shaking both from nervousness and the cold.

"Here," Austin had said, shrugging off his cardigan with heart-shaped elbow pads. "Take this."

"I'm not cold," Jack said, but took it anyway.

"This cardigan is good luck for me," Austin explained. "I wore it all through exams last semester, I wore it during our first investigation... I wore it when I met you." Austin smiled sweetly and Jack's nervousness melted away at the sight. "It's yours."

"Thanks." Jack slipped his arms into the sleeves and immediately felt a prickle of confidence.

Now, Jack picks at the loose thread on the edge of the sleeve. Jack has worn it to every nerve-wracking event since, and today is no exception. As soon as Austin admitted what they were doing that day, Jack dug the cardigan out of his suitcase and shrugged it on, feeling embraced by the warmth of both the knit fabric and Austin's kindness all those years ago.

The second group of fans walks up. This time it's a trio that look to be about their age in their mid-twenties, or maybe a little bit younger.

"Hey, I'm Epiphany," the tallest one introduces themself.

"I'm Darkstar," another says.

"Bug," the third says with a peace sign.

"Let me guess..." Austin says. "Your favorite is Ferris?"

The fans smile and nod.

"My people!" Ferris exclaims. "I'm home!"

A hotel staff member takes one of their phones and Ferris and the fans strike several poses.

"You're my muse," Epiphany tells them.

"Baby... you're *my* muse," Ferris replies.

They hug the three of them and the trio moves on, waving goodbye to the other Ghost Checkers.

"I love them," Ferris says. "So cool."

A couple more groups come by and take pictures with all six of them. Jack notices Lydia and Adeel pretending to be lovey-dovey and rolls his eyes.

The hotel staff member lets another pair of fans through, and two middle-aged women walk up to them, bursting with excitement.

"Cecil Cooper!" one of them exclaims.

"As I live and breathe..." Cecil says. "Kathleen?"

"You know it, sugar!" She walks up to him and hugs him tightly.

"How have you been, honey?" he asks her.

"Oh, right as rain, sweetheart." It's like their southern accents are fighting for dominance.

"Who's this?" Cecil asks, and looks at the second woman.

"How rude of me! Cecil, this is Tammy, my friend from book club I was telling you about."

"Tammy? *The* Tammy? Oh, girl, I've heard so much about you."

Austin looks over at Jack. "I guess they know each other."

Cecil hears him and says, "Oh, do we ever! Guys, this is Kathleen. She has been my biggest fan since I was, what, 19?

And through all that mess in 2017, she never stopped supporting me."

Kathleen waves at the rest of the group. "So ghost hunting, huh? I never expected that from you."

Cecil says, "I never expected it from me, either," and the three of them bust out laughing.

They take a picture, chat for another moment, and the ladies move on.

Another group fangirls over Austin, which is to be expected. His jawline and perfectly coiffed blonde hair are a sure bet for some fangirl tears.

Still, no one has been excited to see Jack yet. Another pair of fans make a beeline for Adeel, which... really? Come on. He's a cameraman intern. But seeing the joy in Adeel's eyes makes Jack smile a bit too. He really deserves this. Adeel was so nervous on the first day of his internship. In addition to destroying what they thought at the time was a 400-year-old statue, Adeel also accidentally deleted an episode's worth of footage, sat on and broke their EVP recorder, and had his thumb in front of the lens for the better part of three hours. It would be easy to wonder why they didn't terminate his internship, but anyone who would wonder that simply hasn't met him. There is a magnetism in his nervous smile, and something about his sweet, chestnut eyes makes the whole world seem okay.

Jack should tell him that.

A few more groups of fans cycle through and Jack finds himself on the sidelines as his friends pose with people who adore them and who barely spare Jack a glance. Cool.

Another group of three fans appears and Jack nods politely at them.

"Jack, hi!" one of the girls says excitedly.

"Hi," Jack says, taken aback.

"Can we get a picture with you?" another of them asks.

"Oh, sure," Jack says, breaking into a smile.

Jack stands in the middle of the backdrop and the three teens wrap their arms around him, huge smiles on their faces. He smiles for the picture and feels that same prickle of confidence in his chest. This cardigan really does work.

The next several groups get pictures with all six Ghost Checkers, and Jack no longer feels left out.

Another fan approaches with her mom. She looks to be about 13, and she looks as nervous as Jack felt at the beginning of all this.

"Go ahead," her mom encourages. "Give it to him."

The little girl walks up to Jack and holds out a bracelet and he gently takes it from her. It's a flat cord with a design woven into it. The background is rainbow, and it has little white skulls dotting the length of it.

"Is this for me?" Jack asks and the girl nods. "You made this?"

She nods again. "It's a friendship bracelet." She lifts her pink jacket sleeve to reveal a matching one.

"What's your name?" he asks her.

"Kayleigh."

"Hi, Kayleigh. I'm Jack."

She giggles and says, "I know."

Jack lays the bracelet over his wrist and says, "Will you tie it for me?"

Kayleigh ties the two loose ends. "There."

"Perfect. I love it." Jack smiles at her. "Thank you. Do you want a picture?"

Kayleigh nods again and her face blooms into a wide smile. She and Jack center themselves in front of the backdrop and her mother snaps a few pictures.

"Thank you for the bracelet. I'm glad we're friends."

Kayleigh smiles and giggles, and she and her mom move on.

The next group of fans obsesses over Lydia and Ferris, and Jack and Austin stand to the side.

"Jeez, I was really starting to think none of these people would like me," Jack says to Austin, who turns to face him fully. Austin looks at him like he didn't understand a word Jack said.

"What?" Jack asks.

"Dude... You're, like, the fan favorite."

"Hardly anyone has even looked at me the whole time."

"Brother, look at the signs."

Jack looks out at the line and for the first time, he takes a moment to read some of the poster board and pieces of cardboard the fans are holding up.

One sign says, "Jack I love you more than pizza". Another has a picture of Jack glued to the cardboard and it proudly proclaims, "I would sell my family for you". He spots a shirt that just features Jack's face. Interesting choice.

A lot of the other signs and shirts are directed towards other team members or the group as a whole, but Jack sees now that a fair share of them are dedicated to him. "I thought our viewers don't really... like me," Jack admits.

Austin looks at him incredulously. "They freaking love you, man. Haven't you read, like, any of the comments?"

"No. I haven't read them in years because of Caty."

"Eh, she's mostly stopped commenting weird stuff. You should take a look at the comments on our most recent video sometime. The people love you, bud."

Jack's glad to hear Caty has simmered down. There for a while, he was considering getting a restraining order. In the end, he decided against it because he figured it would just be another fun challenge for her.

Several more groups of fans pass through, the six of them posing and smiling. Jack doesn't know if it's coming from the cardigan or himself, but he thinks he actually might be starting to have fun. That is, until he sees her.

He spots the sign first: "Jackie I would die for you!" in familiar, jagged handwriting.

He grits his teeth and slowly lowers his gaze to the person's face: mousy brown hair, eyebrows in a permanent scowl, and a smile that feels like spiders crawling on Jack's skin. *Shit.*

"Austin," Jack whispers, but he doesn't hear him. "Austin," he tries again, but Austin is still talking to a fan. He raises his voice a bit more. "Austin!"

"Dude, what?" Austin turns around, exasperated.

"Caty's here."

Austin's face goes lax as he takes it in. "No, that's—No."

Jack points surreptitiously to Caty's sign and Austin slaps a hand onto his forehead.

"Crap."

Jack nods. 'Crap' is right.

"What's going on?" Ferris asks, having noticed Jack's distress.

"That Caty girl we talked about yesterday? She's here."

"Shoot, really? Okay. What's the plan?"

Jack glances at her and accidentally makes eye contact. 'Crap' times ten.

Several more groups of fans come by and Jack feels bad for them because he's certain his smile is not a joyous one.

Caty ends up next in line and Jack feels frozen in place.

"Hi, boys. Been a while," she says with a smile.

"It sure has," Austin says coldly.

"It's so good to meet the new members!" she says, and Jack realizes how long it's been since they last saw her. "We've got Ferris, Lydia, sweet Adeel, and"—her smile glints—"Cecil Cooper."

"That's right," Cecil says with a smile. "And who might you be?"

Caty laughs. "Jack knows who I am. Tell him."

Jack unfreezes and says, "Cecil, this is Caty."

"Oh, jackiesgirl93!" Cecil says. "Pleasure, dear."

Caty smiles at him. "I've seen a lot about you two online recently. I know it's not true, though." She looks at Jack and her eyes glint. "Right?"

"Oh, bless your heart," Cecil says passive aggressively, his honey-sweet tone blanketing his anger. "You're too much."

Caty turns to Jack. "Can I get a picture? For old time's sake?"

"Sure," Jack says with a quick, tight smile.

Caty hands her phone to the staff member and goes to stand next to Jack. She wraps her arm around his back, then lowers it and squeezes just in time for the photo.

Jack jumps away.

Caty laughs. "Missed you, Jackie. Bye, Austin." She holds up a hand and wiggles her fingers.

Jack stands staring at her as she walks away.

"Hey, will you come to the bathroom with me?" Cecil asks and takes Jack's hand to lead him out of the main room.

As soon as the doors close behind them, the drone of the crowd falls away. Jack smells the citrus of a cleaning spray as they pass a custodian, and their footsteps echo in the empty tile-floored hallway.

They get to the entrance to the bathrooms and Cecil gestures to the water fountain. "Do you wanna drink a little? You're pretty pale."

Jack nods wordlessly and takes a few sips from the fountain. When he stands back up, Cecil is looking at him with concern.

"How're you feeling, hon?"

Jack nods. "I'm okay."

"I saw what she did."

Jack feels his face color with embarrassment. He looks away.

"No, Jack, there is nothing to be ashamed of." Cecil grabs Jack's hands and looks up at him. "You didn't do anything wrong, okay? That's unacceptable. They shouldn't have even let her in the event. Didn't they all have to buy tickets?"

"We have an alert set up about her, but she probably used a fake name."

Cecil nods. "That makes me so mad. I'm so sorry that happened, Jack."

"It's okay. She honestly wasn't even that bad this time."

"Wasn't that bad? Jack, that was harassment. You can't tell me it 'wasn't that bad.'"

Jack supposes he's right. That really is what it was. Jack leans against the wall.

"Do you wanna go back up to the room?"

"No, I'm okay. Let's—I wanna finish the event."

"Are you sure?"

Jack picks at the hem of his cardigan again. "Yeah. Let's do it."

Jack was actually starting to have fun before Caty ruined it. This is the first meet and greet he might really enjoy, and he's not going to let her steal the rest of it from him.

They walk back into the room and the remainder of the line cheers. A few groups had hung back and let others go in front of them so they could see Jack and Cecil. Jack smiles. Maybe people do like him.

"You good?" Austin asks. His cheeks are red like they get when he's angry.

"Yeah, I'm fine." Jack smiles, and Austin places a hand on his back.

"I love you, man. I should have said something. I'm sorry."

Jack shakes his head. "It's cool."

Group after group files through and Jack musters a big smile for each of them. They finally they get through the entire line and Jack checks his phone and sees only two and a half hours have gone by. He glances at the merch table, now decimated with just a few lanyards and a poster left. The final group buys it all.

Austin high fives each of the members. "We did it!"

The team cheers, then thanks the hotel staff and heads back up to their room.

As they walk down the quiet hallway, Austin puts a hand on Jack's shoulder and says quietly, "If you need anything, please let me know."

Jack reaches up and squeezes his hand. "You got it."

Cecil catches up to him and says quietly, "That was crazy, huh?"

Jack laughs. "What an understatement." He looks over at Cecil softly. "I'm glad you were there." What Jack means is, *I think I'm starting to feel something and it scares me.*

"Me too, hon."

CHAPTER 11

Austin made sure to place a couple buffer days into the schedule to give the team time to travel and relax a bit. Today is one such day, and the sun is shining so brightly with clouds hanging fluffy in the sky, that Jack could even feel like he's on vacation, were it not for his teammates bickering.

"Dude, what is with your feet?" Ferris says, standing on one of the beds and holding a pillow.

Adeel laughs and lifts his foot. Ferris shrieks and bats it away with the pillow.

"Dude, stop! They're nasty!"

"He's right, Adeel," Cecil says, his shirt collar pulled up over his nose.

"Put those things away," Lydia says, pinching her nose.

"I should be able to be sockless in my own hotel room."

"Not if you want us to get out of here without a fine," Austin says. "Pretty sure the next guests will still be able to smell them too."

"I'm hungry," Jack says quietly.

"Adeel, no!" Ferris yells as Adeel kicks at them. Ferris falls over backwards and bounces once on the bed.

"I'm really hungry," Jack says again, a little louder this time.

"Adeel, leave them alone!" Lydia laughs.

"Can we eat soon?" Jack asks no one.

"Ferris, no. Ferris, no!" Austin says, panicked, as Ferris gets ready to hit Adeel across the face with their pillow.

"Guys, I'm hungry!" Jack shouts. Everyone freezes, Ferris rearing the pillow back, ready to smack Adeel, Austin diving to grab them before they can, Cecil standing nearby, and Lydia standing on the bed for some reason. They all turn and look at Jack, who says quieter, "Can we go eat?"

"How..." Ferris begins, "can you be hungry... with *those* around?" They point at Adeel's feet.

They discuss lunch places for a while before Austin insists they visit a restaurant he found online.

They pull up to a broken-down wooden building with a crooked sign that says, 'Austin's Fry Shack'.

"Really?" Lydia asks.

"Look, guys. It's my restaurant," Austin says, thinking he is much funnier than he is.

"Did you seriously choose this place just because it's your name?" Ferris asks.

"No, I chose it because it must be the best restaurant in all of human history. Austins have good taste."

They walk inside and Austin's claim about good taste does not seem to ring true. There is a huge alligator statue standing in the corner dressed in a baseball jersey. Hundreds of old-timey items decorate the walls. The host is wearing a fish costume.

"Hello," the fish says in a forced-energetic voice. "Welcome to Austin's Fry Shack. How many?"

Austin tells the likely-underpaid fish there are six of them, and the fish leads them to their table in the back corner, bumping into every chair on the way there.

The fish, whose name tag says Monica, places their menus down in front of them and says, "Your server will be right over."

"Austin, you know I'm vegetarian," Lydia says after looking at the meat and seafood-heavy menu.

"I'm sure there's something for you on here," Austin says, scanning for a meatless option. He thumps the laminated menu and says, "Hey, here ya go. Hashbrown casserole."

Lydia frowns. "Alright. Maybe."

Their server, Brandt, arrives and takes their drink orders, then a few minutes later takes their food orders.

Jack orders a fried chicken sandwich. He wishes it were grilled.

Lydia asks, "Is the hashbrown casserole vegetarian?"

Brandt looks confused. "Vegetarian?" He points to the text at the top of the menu: *'All dishes are proudly made with meat.'*

"I'll just stick with water, then." Lydia smiles tightly, then glares at Austin.

Austin orders the Exploding Artery Platter, which includes every type of meat they serve, battered and fried and served on a bed of shredded cheese.

"Will you haunt us when you die from this?" Ferris asks.

"Hey, I eat healthy most of the time."

Cecil orders the Lite Brunch option, which is a fried egg on toast with Canadian bacon.

Lydia perks up and asks, "Can I get that without the bacon?"

"Unfortunately, no," Brandt answers. "It's policy."

Ferris and Adeel each order some kind of fried meat, and Brandt leaves to put in their orders.

Their food arrives soon after, and the team (minus Lydia) digs in.

Jack's sandwich starts dripping some kind of brown liquid. When Brandt walks by, Jack catches him and asks what the sauce is.

Brandt says there is no sauce.

Jack is done with his sandwich.

The team continues eating unknown meat-like substances for a while before Cecil sits back in his chair. Jack can tell something is off.

"You good?" Jack asks quietly.

"I don't feel too well." Cecil looks around. "I'm gonna run to the restroom." He gets up and quickly heads toward the front of the restaurant.

After several minutes, when Cecil has still not returned, Jack decides to go check on him. When he walks into the restroom, he calls, "Cecil? You in here?"

"Yeah," Cecil replies weakly from the first stall.

"You okay?"

Jack hears the lock unlatch and Cecil pushes the stall door open. He's kneeling over the toilet.

"Hi," he says with a weak smile.

"Are you okay?" Jack asks again.

"Yeah, uh... My fried egg? It was *deep fried.*"

Jack's stomach reacts strongly and he bangs another stall door open before gagging over the toilet, coming close to losing his lunch (if one can call it that).

After Jack's stomach settles, he returns to Cecil's stall and places a hand on his shoulder. "Are you ready to stand up? I can take you back to the van."

Cecil nods and takes Jack's hand. He stops at the sink and says, "You should wash your hands, too. I was touching the floor. It's very greasy."

They both wash their hands with weird-smelling soap and Jack helps him out of the bathroom and through the main dining room. Austin spots them and jogs over.

"Hey, you okay?" he asks, concerned.

"Right as rain," Cecil replies. It is not convincing.

"No, 'the best restaurant in human history' made him sick. We're going out to the car. Can I have the keys?"

Austin fishes them out of his pocket and puts them in Jack's hand before saying, "Feel better. We'll pay and be right out."

"Oh, let me give you my wallet—" Cecil says, patting his pockets.

"Don't worry about it, I got it," Austin says. Jack agrees it's the least he can do since it's Austin's fault they're here.

Jack and Cecil walk out to the car, Cecil leaning pretty heavily on his arm. Jack opens the door and Cecil climbs in, resting his head back and closing his eyes. Jack stands leaning in the door.

"Sorry you got sick, Cecil."

"I'm sure I'll be just fine," Cecil says with a smile, eyes still closed, and pats Jack's hand. "I got sicker than this in Houston."

"What happened there?"

"I was poisoned."

"What?"

Cecil laughs. "My tour manager gave me expired yogurt."

A question crosses Jack's mind. "If you're psychic, shouldn't you have known it was spoiled?"

Cecil opens his eyes. "What is this 'if you're psychic' stuff? You said you believe in me now."

"I'm just saying, shouldn't you be able to tell what's going to happen?"

"Jack, I'm a psychic, not an oracle."

"Then shouldn't your guides have told you it was spoiled?"

"What is with this interrogation?"

"I don't know. I guess I'm just still confused about why you know some things and not others. You knew someone was lying to you, but you didn't know the yogurt was spoiled."

"Someone was lying to me?" Cecil repeats. "What do you mean?"

"Your guides, they told you not to trust everything because someone was lying."

"They told me it will be hard to know what's real," Cecil says carefully. "They didn't mention lying. Jack, are my guides talking about you?"

"What? No. I just remembered it wrong."

Cecil eyes him as the rest of the team emerges from the restaurant.

They ride back to the hotel, somehow hitting every pothole and jostling Cecil to no end. Cecil leans on Jack as they make their way up to their room, and as soon as the door opens, Cecil immediately lays down on one of the beds. He still isn't feeling better, and the car ride definitely didn't help.

"Time to review some footage, guys," Austin announces after a while, grabbing his laptop and standing up. "Let's go to the other room so we don't bother Cecil." Ferris, Adeel, and Lydia follow him out.

"You aren't going?" Cecil asks, looking at Jack.

The actual video production process is probably Jack's least favorite part of his job. Thankfully the rest of the team genuinely enjoys it. When it was just Jack and Austin, he had to be much more involved, so this is yet another reason Lydia, Adeel, and Ferris make his life better.

He doesn't like the editing process mainly because it's so... manipulative. They cut it in certain ways so it's more engaging to the viewer, and they leave manufactured cliffhangers before commercial breaks to build suspense. Jack enjoys reviewing recordings to see if they catch any evidence, but he wishes they could just upload videos that are more accurate to the actual investigations. Jack is glad they don't employ much clickbait, but he still isn't quite onboard. "Not my thing," Jack answers simply.

Cecil pats the bed next to him so Jack grabs his book and sits down. After a few minutes, he hears snoring. Jack smiles, then continues reading his book.

After a while, the air conditioning kicks on, waking Jack. He looks over and sees Cecil curled up on his side.

How can such a threat to Jack's world look so harmless?

Jack thinks about his book, now laying open, pages face down on the bed. The scientist has no idea how the alien feels. She's oblivious to the perceived threat she poses, just thinking herself a woman in love.

Jack sighs. Cecil doesn't know he's a threat, does he? Maybe, just for a while, Jack can pretend he's not one.

He shifts so he's further down on the bed and turns to face Cecil's back, not quite touching him. Jack stares at the curly hair on the back of his head. Not a threat. His eyes move lower to the gentle rise and fall of his shoulders. Not a threat.

Slowly, Jack reaches out a hand and ever so slightly touches his arm. Cecil doesn't even stir. Not a threat.

The door unlocks and Jack quickly sits up as it opens. Ferris walks halfway into the room and Jack sees something in their eyes but can't quite identify it. It looks like... panic?

"Jack," they say seriously.

He doesn't know if Ferris pauses ridiculously long, or if time has frozen. Finally, they say, "My mic was on."

CHAPTER 12

It takes Jack a moment to understand what Ferris means. Then it clicks: at Camilla's house, when Jack badmouthed Cecil thinking Ferris's mic was off. Jack grabs Ferris's shoulder and they both step into the hallway.

"You said it was off. At Camilla's, you said it was off."

"I thought it was because it had been acting weird the whole time. But I guess it flicked itself on."

"How much did it catch?"

"All of it." *Shit.*

Jack bites the inside of his lip. He sees Ferris's eyes widen and Jack turns to see Austin marching down the hallway towards them.

"Finch," Austin says and shakes his head. "I am appalled. The way you spoke about our guest... I should remove you from the team."

No. Cecil's message was right. He braces himself for Austin's next words.

"If I didn't love you like a brother, I would. But Jack, man, I told you several times you can't act that way. Fucking stop it."

What? He's not kicked out? "I'm sorry. I will."

"You said that last time." Austin tries to push past him but Jack gets in his way, blocking the hotel room door.

"Please, you can't show him." Jack looks at Austin, searching his eyes for understanding. "Please."

Austin makes a face. "Show him? And have our one hope leave the tour? No, I'm not that stupid." Austin sighs. "But I can't promise Lydia or Adeel won't show him." Austin pushes past him and Jack tenses. "I'm just going to the vending machine, relax. I don't even have my laptop, how would I show him?"

His laptop. If Jack can get to Austin's laptop and delete the footage, he can bypass this whole mess. He leaves Ferris in the hallway and half-jogs to the other room and knocks on the door.

Lydia opens it and crosses her arms. "What do you want?"

"Lydia, please, I can't have him see this."

"He deserves to know."

"Then tell him yourself. But please don't show him." Jack takes a breath. "I said some hurtful things in there. Please don't do that to him."

Lydia drops her arms. "You did say hurtful things. What happened? I thought you were starting to like him."

"I was. He's a nice guy."

"Then what are your real feelings for him?"

That's a good question. At first, he hated him. Then he got to know him, so he hated him a little less. But when he realized Cecil was flirting, things got more... complicated. Just a few minutes ago, when life was peaceful, and all Jack had to worry about was waking him up by accident, he could even think he might like him in a different way. A deeper way.

"I don't know, Lydia. I haven't really felt this way before." Jack's eyes search the middle distance for his next words. "It's like... any way I feel, I feel better when I'm with him. Even yesterday, with Caty and everything, he made it all better. I thought I hated him before, but I don't, I— I really, really like him. And I don't know, maybe there's something to those rumors. Maybe there is something between us." Jack pauses, then says, "But none of that even matters if Cecil hears that recording. Please."

Lydia frowns. "I'm sorry, Jack. We already sent it."

Sent it? What does she mean 'sent it?'

Jack notices Austin's laptop on the table, Austin's Gmail open on the screen. He looks at her, then at Adeel. "No," he breathes.

Jack races back to the other hotel room, and as soon as he's close enough to hear voices through the door still hanging ajar, he knows it's too late.

"You can still be friends—"

"Did you *hear* him? I'm a psychic. 'We can never be friends.' And to think I flirted with that boy." There is a pause, and Jack hears, "I shouldn't have wasted my time with this tour."

Jack hears suitcase wheels and Cecil appears in the doorway.

"Hello," Jack says, because it's all he can say.

"Hi." Cecil looks into Jack's eyes as if asking a question, and when he doesn't find his answer, or at least the answer he wants, Jack sees him shatter.

He watches as Cecil disappears down the hallway.

Jack turns and walks in to see Ferris standing in the middle of the room.

"Jack..." Ferris starts, "what have you done?"

"I should have stopped you," Ferris says a while later as they all sit solemnly in the hotel room. "I should have told you not to say those things. I was there. I could have stopped this."

"Don't blame yourself..." Lydia says gently. "Blame Jack." She glares at him from across the room.

"I'm sorry," Jack says for the thousandth time in the last hour.

"Guys, there's nothing we can do about it now. It happened, and that's it. It sucks, but it's not like Jack did it on purpose. So let's just try to move on." Austin starts discussing how this impacts the rest of the tour.

Jack walks to the window. He has bitten the inside of his cheek to shreds. He can't stop thinking about Cecil's message. It's the day before the eighth stop, and Jack didn't lose the group. So he succeeded, right? He accepted that Cecil was part of the group. That's what he was supposed to do. Everything is supposed to be okay. Why does he feel like he's lost everything? All he's lost is Cecil.

Cecil, who had found every way to make Jack laugh in such a short period of time. Cecil, who was always in a good mood, even when he didn't feel well. Cecil, whose laugh could light up the sky. Cecil, who had grown dear to him.

Jack's world freezes. The trees stop swaying outside. The radiator stops buzzing. It all stands still.

The thing dear to him wasn't the group at all, but Cecil. And he just watched him leave.

But how? He had done his best to accept Cecil's presence. He should have succeeded.

Jack closes his eyes and thinks back through the last 12 days, trying to pinpoint where he went wrong. He thinks about what he said in the recording and opens his eyes. He insisted psychics aren't real. They aren't. Unless...

Unless that's what he's supposed to accept: that maybe there are things he can't understand.

A familiar fear rises in his throat. Jack recognizes it from every time he didn't understand something, couldn't understand something. It stems from his father's advice: 'the more you understand, the less afraid you will be.' The flip side that Jack had come to learn is: *what cannot be understood should be feared.'*

Jack is not afraid of Cecil. He never has been afraid of Cecil. He's been afraid of the unknown surrounding him. That must be why Jack's grandmother told him he needs to accept him.

But the harm is already done. Cecil is already gone, and the heavy ache has already settled deep in Jack's chest. There is nothing he can do now.

The rest of the day passes slowly, tension starting to unravel between Jack and the rest of the team. He knows it has dissolved when Lydia offers him some of her tofu. She never does that because she knows how much he hates it. It must be a test.

Jack takes the fork and tastes it. It's gross, but Jack thanks her, and she smiles. He must have passed.

They send Jack for pizza later that evening. Normally he would object, but he knows they're testing how sorry he is, so he goes without complaint.

The drive to the pizza place is silent. Jack doesn't deserve music. Cecil liked music.

Jack is waiting in line in the small restaurant when he feels his phone buzz in his pocket. He doesn't deserve to check it. Cecil liked checking his phone.

He grabs the three pizza boxes and heads back out to the car. His phone starts buzzing again. It could be one of the members of the team. He looks at it, but it isn't a number he recognizes.

"Hello?"

"Jack," his father says. "I'm calling from the hospital. It's your aunt." For the second time that day, the world stops.

CHAPTER 13

Jack barely even says goodbye to the team. He can hardly bring himself to speak. He just throws yesterday's clothes back into his suitcase and rushes to his rideshare already waiting outside, telling his friends he'll explain later.

Jack settles into the cushy black leather backseat of the car after confirming the destination with the driver. He watches the downtown skyline zoom past.

Jack opens the team's group chat and sees Cecil has already removed himself. He texts the group: *Mel is sick. Had to rush to airport. Talk soon.* He types out *'I love you'* but deletes it, not feeling that he deserves to use those words after ruining their chances at saving the show. If he hasn't shown them the love they deserve, saying it in a text is meaningless.

The airport is a long drive away. Jack bites his nails down to the bed. And because it's just Jack's luck, they get stuck in traffic.

54 minutes into what should have been a 40-minute drive, Jack thinks about something Ferris had said about chanting. Jack has no basis to believe it works, but he'll try anything to save his aunt, so he starts chanting silently, barely moving his lips. "She'll be okay, she'll be okay, she'll be okay."

They get through the slow-down and finally arrive at the airport. Jack thanks the driver, grabs his bag, and rushes to the entrance.

He stands in line to speak to an associate for what feels like hours, bouncing his foot and staring into the middle distance. Finally it's Jack's turn and he purchases a one-way ticket to Florida. He checks his suitcase and heads to the gate.

Of course there are security slow-downs. Why wouldn't there be? The line fills the winding queue space and extends far into the lobby of the airport. Jack hikes to the end of the line and waits.

And waits.

And waits.

The line barely moves for half an hour, and the people in front of him lean over or stand on their toes, trying to see what's holding everyone up.

TSA must have opened a few more security lanes because the line finally starts moving slowly but surely, and when Jack is around 20 people away, he spots the cause of the hold-up.

There is a young couple with two young children who look about 4 and 6. The older, their daughter, has her arms crossed and her face crumpled into a scowl. The family has been moved out of the way to a closed line.

The little girl stomps her foot. "No."

The woman looks at the TSA officer helplessly, but no sympathy crosses his face.

Jack listens for a moment, piecing together what happened.

Apparently, the daughter's grandmother had given her a bottle of 'fairy magic', which looked to be some kind of sparkly liquid, but the container exceeded 3.4 ounces, so they needed to toss it or miss their flight.

"Sweetie, we can get you more."

"Grammy gave this to me!"

"Get more from grammy," the TSA officer says, clearly just wanting them out of his line.

"I can't." The little girl crosses her arms and scrunches her face.

The father turns to the TSA officer and says pleadingly, "Sir, her grandma just died, we're going down for her funeral, and this is pretty much all she has left of her. We had no idea she brought it. Please."

The officer doesn't waiver.

Jack sees the desperation on the family's face. Cecil would know what to do. He'd probably contact the kid's grandmother (if that's possible, or at least he'd pretend). Jack wishes he could do something helpful too. Then he has an idea.

"Excuse me, sorry, thank you." Jack passes the rest of the people in line to reach the family.

The officer holds up his hand and says, "Sir, get back in line."

"I will, I just—I think I can help?"

Jack shrugs off his backpack and drops it on the floor. He unzips it and rummages around.

"Sir, the line is moving." Sure enough, people who were only a few spots in front of Jack are moving through security now.

"Here it is," Jack says, producing an empty travel-size bottle. "I had this extra one. It's 3 ounces. Maybe you can pour some of the fairy... uh, fairy stuff in here?" he says to the little girl, holding out the lime green translucent bottle.

She eyes him uncertainly, then looks at the bottle. She reaches out to take it and says, "Okay."

The whole family breathes a sigh of relief.

"We still have..." the man checks his watch, "23 minutes before boarding ends. Thank you so much, sir," he says to Jack.

"Yes, thank you," the woman says, relief plain on her face.

"No problem." Jack turns and looks for his place in line, but sees no one he recognizes. "Um..."

"Back of the line."

Jack looks at the TSA officer. "What? I just helped you."

The man shakes his head. "You aren't in line. Get in line."

Jack, in disbelief, walks to the back of the line. Thankfully it's moving faster than it was when he first stood in this spot, but he's still fuming, nevertheless.

Jack reaches the front of the line, makes it through security and heads to the gate.

Jack's heart falls when he sees he missed his boarding window. He rushes to the desk and the woman tells him the plane is already gone.

He buys a standby ticket for the next flight which is leaving in two hours, and takes a seat to wait. He reads on and off, but can't focus for more than a minute or two at a time. He can't stop thinking of Mel. How long has she been so sick? Probably a lot longer than anyone knows.

Jack takes deep breaths and tries to settle his climbing heartrate. He glances around at all the people rushing by: families with kids trailing behind them, groups of older women with matching cruise t-shirts on, individuals by themselves engrossed in their laptops. They're all so lucky. As far as Jack can tell from this far away, their hearts are still in their bodies. Jack is holding his in his hand, cradling it, as it comes dangerously close to shattering. But Mel will be okay. She has to be.

Finally, they call his zone and Jack boards his flight. He checks his phone over and over for updates from his father until the flight attendants say to put electronics on airplane mode.

She'll be okay, she'll be okay, she'll be okay, he chants silently to himself. His ears pop painfully as they take off, but he couldn't care less.

A couple hours later, the pilot announces their descent, and as soon as they land, Jack turns his data back on. He has seven missed calls from his father. He cradles his phone in both hands and can't do anything but breathe.

Jack calls him and shakily lifts the phone to his ear.

"Jack."

"We just landed. Dad…" Jack waits with bated breath, but knows what his father is going to say.

"I'm sorry, son."

And just like that, a part of him is ripped out. Every breath is hard to draw. *No, no, no.*

"When?" Jack asks.

"About an hour ago."

Jack pulls his phone away from his face for a moment and looks at the time. An hour ago. If that TSA officer had let him go through, he could have been home hours ago in time to see her. He could have been with her.

Jack wasn't there. Mel died and he wasn't there. He wonders if she was lucid enough to notice. He remembers his father is still on the phone and says, "Sorry, uh... Sorry." Jack's mind is full of a grief-colored fuzz and nothing makes any sense. His chest starts aching with every breath and his eyes prick with tears.

"I'll see you soon?" Jack's father asks.

"I... yeah. See you soon."

The call ends with a beep.

The passengers all stand at once and grab their bags in a frenzy, eager to get off the plane. Jack stays sitting still. He is no longer in a rush.

His seat is towards the back of the plane, so he lets everyone else file off before he even unbuckles his seatbelt.

A flight attendant walks past him with a broom and stops when she sees him. "Sir? Are you okay?"

Jack nods and stands up before walking down the long aisle.

He doesn't even know how he got to baggage claim but he's vaguely aware of his suitcase coming around the carousel. He makes no move to grab it.

It comes around a second time and he walks up to it, but isn't fast enough. Jack is moving through a wall of water, every movement slow, difficult, impossible.

When it comes around a third time and he still can't grab it, an older woman next to him says, "I'll help you, honey." It cycles through a fourth time, and she grabs it and sets it down next to him.

Jack looks at her. Her eyes are creased at the outer corners, and there are deep lines by her mouth. Her hair is gray and curly, most of it clipped back but some of it escaping in wild ringlets like fire escaping a star. She wears a bold shade of purple lipstick, and it makes her smile look even brighter as she looks at him.

"Are you okay, sweetheart?"

Jack nods but can't stop looking at her. She looks just like Mel. His eyes sting.

"Oh, sweetie, come here." She brings him into a hug. "Today is a hard day, huh?"

Jack nods, and he can't keep it together any longer. He brings his arms up and clutches onto her, feeling the soft quilted fabric of her vest. She rubs his back, wooden bangles clattering together, and he closes his eyes. Jack could almost pretend he's hugging his aunt, could almost pretend he's just standing in her kitchen and everything is okay again, but a loud message about unattended baggage breaks the spell.

Jack pulls back from her and quickly wipes his eye. "Sorry," he says to the complete stranger whose arms he just broke down in.

"Nothing to be sorry for." The woman glances at her watch. "I have to go. Are you going to be okay?"

Jack nods, wiping another tear. He isn't sure.

He watches her walk away, dragging a huge zebra print suitcase behind her. He lets out a wet laugh. That's exactly what Mel would choose, too. Jack's smile drops as he watches the woman disappear around a corner. He's lost her again.

Jack sighs deeply and wipes his cheek on the back of his hand one final time before pulling up his suitcase handle and stepping out into the soupy, Florida air.

The drive to the house is excruciating. The ride cost him $68 to book but he didn't even blink at the price. Jack just wants to get home.

The car stops and Jack looks up to see his childhood home. He thanks the driver and grabs his luggage from the trunk before the car drives off.

He takes a deep breath and walks across the stepping stones, weeds grown up around them. He reaches the front door and knocks. As he waits, he notices a dirt dauber nest above the door, and orange streaks coming down from the gutter. Paint is chipping on the doorframe. The house has aged just like he has.

His first cousin Terri opens the door with a sad smile.

"Hi, Jackie."

"Hey, Ter."

"Come on in."

Jack steps inside and toes off his shoes by the front door. Mel's rule.

He walks further into the house and Terri steps into the kitchen. Jack looks around and sees various families milling around Mel's house. Uncles and aunts he hasn't seen in years, distant cousins and their spouses who probably never even met her.

Jack turns to walk down the hallway towards his old room when he collides with his father who reaches out his hands to steady him.

"Jack," he says. "Good to see you."

Jack smiles halfheartedly.

"You can drop your bags in your room and join us in the dining room. We're about to have dinner."

Jack's room is exactly how he remembers it. Bunk beds with bright red bedding, dusty accordion closet doors that never quite close all the way, and a cross-stitch Mel made that says *Jackie's Room*. Mel even kept his stuffed rhino.

Jack sits on the bed and picks it up. It's just as soft as it used to be, but Jack does remember it being bigger.

He hugs the rhino and sighs. Mel did so much for him. He hopes she knew how grateful he was. Is. Was?

Jack sits this way for a long time. He's still hugging his rhino and staring at a photo of Mel and himself when Jack's father leans in the door.

"Jack? You ready for dinner?"

Jack feels like a kid again. He always had a very emotional stomach. If anything was bothering him even the slightest bit, he would feel too sick to eat. Jack doesn't want to come to the table, but he's an adult now and he needs to. He doesn't know why, but he knows that's what's expected of him. Jack thinks it should be socially acceptable for adults to hide from situations like this, too.

Jack walks out and takes his seat at the table between his father and Terri.

His uncle Cletus stands and says, "Now that we're all here, let's say grace."

Jack glances around. Is no one going to object? Mel wasn't Christian. Why would she want him to say grace in her home?

Jack keeps his mouth shut and listens to Cletus say some wishy-washy, sugar coated prayer about how happy Mel is now that she's with Jesus. Bullshit. Mel would be happier here with her family, with him.

Jack hates that he doesn't know where she is. He doesn't know what happened to her. Is she just some drifting spirit now? Will he see a shell of her staring blankly when he opens his eyes in the middle of the night?

Jack picks at his dinner and as soon as it is proper, he gets up and heads back to his room. He sits down on his bed again, one knee up, the other leg hanging off, the ball of his foot bouncing on the floor. His phone feels like a heavy weight in his pocket. Jack pulls it out and sighs.

Jack

Hey. Mel died. I'm at her house with the rest of my family.

Austin

I am so sorry, jack. please let us know if you need anything

Lydia

jack thats awful :((yes pls let us know

Ferris

we love you jack!!! we're here for u!!

Adeel

Sorry for your loss :)

Shoot I meant :(

He texts again a second later:

Adeel

I'm so sorry

Jack chuckles.

Jack

Thanks guys. Love you all

When he looks up, he nearly drops his phone, startled to see Terri standing in the doorway.

"Sorry, didn't mean to scare you."

"No, you're fine."

She walks further into the room and sits on the lower bunk next to him. She picks up the rhino and puts it in her lap. "Cute. Was this yours?"

"Yeah. Mel gave it to me when I moved in here."

"Oh, yeah. I always forget you guys lived here."

Terri is much older than Jack, and was already out of the house by the time Jack and his father moved in when Jack was seven.

"Crazy she's gone."

"Yeah," Terri agrees.

"I can't believe I wasn't here. Some stupid tour..."

To Jack's surprise, Terri laughs. "Stupid tour? Jack, do you have any idea how excited she was about it? It's all she would talk about for a while. *You're* all she would talk about."

"Really?"

"Yeah. Even just a few days ago when family was first arriving, she was making sure to tell everyone about it and even showed us the first few videos that are up."

"That's sweet." *Wait...* "A few days ago? Why did family get here a few days ago?"

Terri grimaces. "Jack..."

"You all knew she was sick and no one told me?"

Terri matches his volume. "She didn't *want* us to tell you." Quieter, she says, "She told us if we interrupted your work, she would whoop us. Her words."

That does sound like Mel. Her whole life, she never would admit to how sick she was or how much pain she was in. Others were always her priority. Everyone else always took precedence in her life.

"Why?" Jack asks. He grabs his rhino.

"She loved you and loved your work. She didn't want to get in the way of that."

"She wouldn't have been getting in the way. Did she not know how much I love her, how important she was to me?"

"It's just her nature. Of course she knew you loved her. Everyone loved her. She just loved everyone more." Terri places a hand on Jack's arm and squeezes.

They sit side by side in silence for a while. Jack has no concept of how much time has passed. He only knows there's just not enough of it.

CHAPTER 14

The next few days are a blur, yet they pass at a crawl. Most of the family are staying at nearby hotels, so it's just Terri, Jack, and his father, Keith, in the house most of the time.

Terri has tried many career fields, including medical, legal, artistic, and what Jack is most thankful for: culinary. This week, she has been cooking them the most delicious gourmet comfort foods and Jack could not be more grateful.

Whenever Jack was sick or upset, Mel would make him mashed potatoes from scratch with just the right level of chunkiness. As soon as he mentioned this to Terri, all their meals started including mashed potatoes, made almost exactly how Mel used to do it.

"What a week," Jack's father says from his place at the head of the table.

"What a week," Terri repeats.

"Memorial is coming up," Jack's father reminds everyone.

Oh yeah. That. Jack is not looking forward to that.

The conversation moves on, and Terri says, "Sorry you're missing your tour, Jackie."

"They actually aren't continuing it. Two of us already left, so it'd be kinda hard."

"Two? Who else left?"

"Oh, it was a guy named Cecil. He's a psychic from the internet."

"Oh, oh," she snaps her fingers, then remembers the name: "Coopernatural! Right? Is that him?"

"Yeah. You've heard of him?"

"Yes, he did a reading for Gerry Griffin a long, long time ago. You know, that talk show host? He outed her for having an affair with her pool boy." Mel laughs. "Oh, he was so young then. What is he now, twenty?"

"Twenty-six."

"Oh, jeez, I'm old." Everyone but Jack laughs.

Jack wonders where Cecil is now. He didn't say where he was going, but he probably went home to Boston. Jack sighs. He wonders if he's still upset.

The days continue to pass, and the family starts going through Mel's things. Jack's skin crawls at the thought of invading her privacy like that, so he spends most of the day in his old room ignoring texts from people who love him.

The team has been texting him every day, but they understand he doesn't have the energy to reply, and they don't mind.

It's mainly updates about what they're doing. For example:

Ferris

i just dyed lyd's hair omg it looks so bad

Lydia

WHAT??? u said it looked good wtf

Ferris

no it's so bad it's good, u look cute i promise uwu

Austin

Ok the truth is ferris *bleached* lydia's hair and it is now very yellow

But she kind of rocks it

Lydia

ty

Jack smiles. He loves these people with all his heart. He sighs as he puts his phone down, the energy to reply simply not within him.

"Jack," his father calls from the other room, "come help with these boxes."

Thinking his father just needs help lifting them, he emerges from his room, but quickly discovers that he means for Jack to go through them.

Jack's father and Terri are sitting on the couch, cardboard boxes in front of them. They're sorting Mel's belongings into three bins, presumably Keep, Donate, and Discard.

"No, I can't—I can't do that."

"Sure you can. Pull up a chair. Start with this one." He points to the box to his right.

Jack sits slowly and reaches into the box. His hands shaking, he picks up a ceramic dog. It used to sit on her mantle. Jack glances up at it and sees it bare, just a slab of rock above the fireplace, free of all Mel's knick-knacks. This just doesn't feel right.

Jack stares at the dog figurine in his hand. It reminds him of Lydia's. He smiles and decides to snap a picture and send it to the group.

Immediately his friends respond.

Lydia

IT LOOKS LIKE POPPYYYY

Ferris

omg so cute

Austin

Love and miss you man

Jack's smile grows.

"Hey, off your phone," his father instructs. "Focus."

"Sorry," Jack mutters, feeling like a kid again.

After a few boxes and a few hours go by, Jack is emotionally exhausted. The simple act of reaching into the box is taxing, and appraising her items is becoming impossible. It all deserves to be kept. It was Mel's.

Jack's tired eyes prick with tears and he rests his forehead in his hand. He doesn't expect the sob that wracks him.

"Oh, Jackie," Terri says with concern.

"C'mere, son," Jack's father says, hauling him into a hug. Jack clutches at him and fights to breathe, the still air of this house no longer filling his lungs enough.

"Go take a break, Jack," his father instructs, patting him on the shoulder.

Jack goes straight back to his room, grabs his rhino, and cries. Tears fall freely and he doesn't bother wiping them away, each droplet one last connection to Mel.

After what simultaneously feels like hours and seconds, Jack takes a deep, shuddering breath and the sobs slowly stop.

He sighs and gazes around his room, trying to remember how it felt to live here. He looks at the cross stitches Mel made for him, and the height marks on his closet door frame. Jack glances at the top of the closet and frowns.

Is it really still here? He stands and grabs it off the top shelf: his dad's old EMF meter. Jack had no idea what happened to it after he moved out. He should have known Mel had kept it for him.

He sits back down on the bed and holds the small black box in his hand. It has two silver sensors sticking out of the front, with two light bulbs—one green, one red—and an ON switch sticking out of the top.

Jack's dad had made this with his own hands.

Jack is lucky his family believes in ghosts. He knows a lot of people reject the idea as a whole. If Jack had seen the man in the suit and met nothing but rejection from his family, he doesn't know what he would have done. If his family hadn't banished the ghost for him, Jack would have either had to switch rooms or live in fear.

There is a knock on his door before the handle turns and it slowly opens to reveal his father peering in.

"Hey bud," he says as he opens the door all the way. "How're ya doin'?"

Jack sniffles and wipes at his eyes. "Fine."

He sits down on the bottom bunk next to him and pats Jack's knee. "You can talk to your old man, you know." He sighs and says, "I know we haven't always been the closest, and I'm sorry if I've ever made you feel like you can't talk to me, but I want you to know you can." He catches Jack's eyes and smiles.

Jack thinks about Mel, and the aching in his chest that hasn't gone away since he got that first phone call. He wonders if she's haunting the house now, if he'll open his eyes and see her drifting from closet to wall. Would she even recognize him?

He feels tears prick at his eyes again, and his throat constricts. At least then he'd get to see her again. Feel her presence again.

He wishes he could talk to her just one more time.

Jack looks down at the EMF meter in his hands.

"Dad," Jack begins. "Do you remember when you gave me this?" He holds up the EMF meter and his father takes it gently and chuckles.

"Yes, I do."

Jack glances over at his father and notices how old he looks. He has wrinkles radiating out from the corners of his tired eyes, and there is a puffiness below them. Jack wonders if he's been crying.

"You started to say something. Back then, when you gave this to me," Jack says, watching him carefully. "I think you were going to tell me about when you made this."

His father nods his head slightly and settles back into the bunk. "Son," he begins. "When your mother died, I wanted to do anything I could to speak to her again. I was barely into my twenties, and I was by myself with a newborn. I needed all the help I could get and"—his breath hitches—"I just needed her."

Jack can't meet his eyes.

"I found this medium in my town who claimed she could contact her, so I made an appointment and went in and..."

"And she was a fake?"

Jack's father smiles sadly. "No. She was anything but." He takes a deep breath and gazes into the middle distance. "She contacted her and knew things only your mom would know. She talked about how we met, our first date, our wedding..." He chuckles, but his eyes grow heavier and cloudy. "I went back every week." He pauses for a long moment, then seems to come back to himself, and his eyes are clearer when he looks at Jack again. "I went back every week for months. It consumed me, the idea that I could still talk to her. Your aunt

Mel is the one that helped me out of it, ironically enough. She talked sense into me, and that's when I made the meter. It was a way for me to contact her by myself, to know she was there, without having to lose myself in it."

Jack frowns. "All this time you've told me spirits can't be contacted… you were lying?"

"No, I—You have to understand, I didn't want you going down the same path I did—"

"All this time psychics have been real?"

Jack's father stays quiet, looking at him sadly.

Jack turns away and stares at the chocolate milk stain that never came out of the carpet.

His father places a hand on his back. "Sorry, bud. I just wanted to do what was best for you."

"You don't know what's best for me." Jack has wasted weeks hating Cecil for lying when he could have accepted him from the start, could have been friends from the start. Who knows what could have developed in that time had his father's words not been stuck in his head?

"I'll leave you be." Jack's dad rises slowly from the bed and straightens. "Terri's making sandwiches for lunch." He closes the door behind him.

Jack glances at his phone and chews on his lip. So talking to Mel again is possible?

Jack lets out a sigh. There is no way he can call Cecil, no way he can ask him to contact Mel. Jack can't possibly ask him to do that. Not now, not after he hurt him.

But if there is the slightest chance he could speak to Mel again, isn't it worth it?

Jack eyes his phone. He thinks about his father, and the way he lost himself to that psychic medium, but then the grief squeezes his heart again and before he can change his mind, he darts his hand out to grab his phone off the bed.

It rings for a moment before Cecil answers. "Hello?"

"Hi," Jack says simply.

"Oh, Jack," Cecil says, surprised. His tone hardens. "What do you want?"

"I—" Jack begins, but a sob comes out of nowhere.

"Oh, goodness. Um, what's—what's going on?" Cecil asks, voice filling with panic.

"My aunt, she—My aunt."

"Oh, Jack." Cecil tuts his tongue. "I'm sorry to hear that."

"I just..." Jack steels himself for his next words. "I just want to talk to her again."

Cecil sighs on the other end. "Where are you?" Jack tells him the name of his town and Cecil says, "I'll come down. I'll be there, uh... today, okay? Text me your address."

Jack sniffles and says, "Okay." They're silent for a moment, and Jack says, "Thank you."

"Of course, Jack Finch."

True to his word, Cecil arrives that night around 9 PM. He shows up at the door in rumpled clothes with one small duffel bag slung over his shoulder.

"Where are the rest of your bags?"

"I didn't have much time to pack. Just a carry-on for me."

"Cecil, you really didn't have to rush—"

Cecil holds up a hand to silence him. "When Jack Finch asks for help, you help. Even I know that." Terri steps into the entryway and Cecil says animatedly, "Hello! I'm Cecil. You must be Terri. Oh, look at you! Yellow is definitely your color, hon!"

Terri and Cecil immediately hit it off, and even Jack's dad seems to like him. They saved Cecil some dinner, which he eats happily at the kitchen table while the rest of them make conversation.

"So, Cecil," Jack's father starts, and Jack tenses. He doesn't know why he feels like a teen bringing a boyfriend home. "You're a psychic, huh?"

"Yes, I am, sir." Cecil grabs another roll.

"Where did you study?" Jack's dad asks, thinking he's being funny.

It doesn't trip Cecil up, though. He says, "Learned on the job, sir. I had my first psychic experience at seven and predicted my mother's pregnancy, then I did my first reading at nine years old, and it all snowballed from there."

The family asks him a few more questions about his work. Then the conversation shifts to his family.

"I was practically raised by my grandmother. My father was an ass and my mother died when I was pretty young."

"How many siblings do you have?" Terri asks.

"Only child right here."

Terri looks confused. "But your mother's pregnancy?"

"Oh." Cecil stops eating. "She... lost the pregnancy." He keeps his eyes firmly on his plate.

"Sorry to hear that," Terri says. "That's hard as a kid. For anyone, but, especially when you're so young."

Cecil smiles politely but Jack can see the tightness in his eyes. "Yes, it is." He finishes eating and Jack shows him to the guest bedroom.

It's a small room with light pink walls and several cross-stitches of geese.

"Oh, these are just darling!" Cecil exclaims.

"You can have 'em."

"What, you don't want them?" Cecil asks, turning around to face Jack.

"We can't keep everything. I'd rather they go to you than some thrift store."

Cecil looks at the geese again and says, "Well in that case, yes, I'd be delighted." He puts his bag down by the bed. "Did she make those? Mel?"

"Probably. Her or Terri."

"I like Terri," Cecil says, beginning to unpack.

"Sorry she asked you that back there."

"Oh, it ain't nothing."

Jack sits on the bed next to where Cecil is lining up his toiletries. He says softly, "It didn't seem like nothing."

Cecil straightens and looks at him, then smiles and sits down. "No, you're right. It's not nothing." Cecil sighs. "When

I was seven, I woke up with a knowingness that my mother was pregnant. At seven, I don't even think I knew what pregnancy really was. And so I told my mother, she took a test, and I was right. She was so happy." He smiles wistfully, then looks down at his shoes. "I didn't tell her the rest of what I knew. I didn't want to stop her from being happy."

Jack cocks his head, wordlessly encouraging him to continue.

"A few months later, she went to the ER with stomach pain." Cecil looks at Jack and smiles sadly. "She lost the baby. My grandmother found out I knew from the start and told me it was my fault." He laughs bitterly. "She said if I had told them what I knew when I found out, they could have saved the baby."

"You were *seven*," Jack says in disbelief.

"I know." Cecil sighs and says again, "I know."

"That's so not fair to put on a kid."

"But that's the thing about being psychic. You know things that affect people, and you have to make the hard decision of figuring out what to tell them. Do I break someone's heart now, or let them wander into that same heartbreak later?" Cecil sighs. "I never wanted to be psychic."

"Really?"

"Oh, yeah. No. My parents took me to psychologist after psychologist asking what was wrong with me. Nothing ever was wrong with me except... me. My nature. My '*abilities*,'" he says, mocking himself. "Abilities. More like a curse, sometimes."

Jack hadn't realized Cecil was carrying such a burden. He always carries himself so happily, like he's just floating through life. No one can really float with a weight like that on their shoulders.

"Sorry," Cecil says, back to his usual bright self. "I shouldn't have dumped all that on you. I'm here for *you*. Sorry, Jack."

"No, you have nothing to be sorry for. *I'm* sorry." Jack takes a breath. "You know I didn't mean any of that, right? On the recording?"

Cecil eyes him.

"I didn't. I think I was just scared or—or angry, or something. I don't know. Of course you're my friend.

Cecil gives him a sad smile. "Ok, hon. Well, I'm just gonna..." He gestures to his belongings spread out on the bed.

"Oh, yes, you unpack. I'll see you in the morning." Jack stands and walks toward the door.

"Bright and early!"

Jack chuckles. "We'll see about that. You just got in from a flight."

"Nothin' stops me from rising early, Jack Finch."

Jack laughs again. It feels... normal again. But Jack knows it's not. It never will be.

CHAPTER 15

In the morning, Jack wakes up to the smell of bacon. As far as his mornings have gone this week, that's not such a bad way to wake up.

He sleepily wanders into the kitchen, still in his sleep pants, and finds Cecil at the stove.

"Good morning," Cecil says brightly.

"Morning," Jack replies, stifling a yawn. Jack sees Terri at the breakfast bar and his father in the armchair in the living room. Jack sits in the third barstool next to Terri.

He notices Cecil is wearing a frilly apron. "Is that Mel's?"

"Yes," Cecil says. He hurriedly adds, "Terri told me it'd be fine to use it, but I can take it off if—"

"No," Jack says and smiles. "It kinda suits you."

"Well, that's quite a compliment." He smiles and turns back to the stove.

Cecil is stirring scrambled eggs and has bacon sizzling in another pan, but Jack smells something sweet too. His eyes follow the scent to the waffle iron.

"So you *can* make waffles."

Cecil scoffs sassily and turns around. "I can when it's a normal waffle iron." He turns back around and mutters, "What kind of waffle iron flips over? That's not how god intended it."

"Did I miss something?" Terri asks, amused.

"Cecil doesn't know how to—"

"I am not a fan of those silly hotel waffle irons. The ones that flip? Not into it." Cecil waves his spatula in the air dismissively.

Terri laughs. "Bet you encountered a lot of those on the road. So how come you left the tour, Cecil?"

Cecil doesn't turn around. He clicks his tongue, then says, "I had something I needed to take care of."

Jack hates that he felt the need to lie. Jack is done with lying. "No, actually," Jack begins, and Cecil glances at him over his shoulder. "I said some really hurtful things about him and he found out. It was my fault completely."

Eggs finished, Cecil sets them aside and turns around, leaning on the counter. He gives Jack an appraising look and smiles. "Your cousin's a meanie," he jokes to Terri.

"He got it from me," she says. "Isn't that right Jackie-poo?" She catches him around the neck and ruffles his hair.

Jack rolls his eyes but can't stop the smile that spreads across his face.

He catches Cecil's eyes and Cecil smiles softly. It looks a whole lot like forgiveness.

The day passes slowly in a haze, and that evening, Jack and Cecil are sitting on the couch when Cecil says, "So..."

Jack doesn't like his tone and braces himself for his next words.

"You called me here for a reason. Do you... still want to do that?"

Oh. Jack had contacted him to talk to Mel. But sometimes he can pretend she's just in the other room, or she's out grocery shopping and will be back soon. To talk to her as a ghost will solidify her absence. Until then, Jack can pretend. But he knows it's time.

"Yeah." Jack clears his throat. "Where's the best place for that?"

"Wherever you're comfortable. Is there somewhere Mel loved, maybe?"

Jack instantly knows where to go.

"This is beautiful," Cecil says in awe, gazing around at the old oak trees, their trunks wrapped in white Christmas lights. They line the pedestrian walking mall which extends several blocks.

"Maybe here?" Cecil suggests, pointing to a nearby bench. It's situated right under one of the largest trees, its branches encircled by sparkling white light.

They sit together silently as Cecil gazes up at the tree. "Wow," he breathes.

"You like trees, huh?"

"I do." Cecil goes quiet again and Jack could almost believe he'd gotten up and walked off if he couldn't feel the warmth from Cecil's thigh next to his own. Finally, Cecil says, "I was thirteen when my mother died."

Jack gapes at the sudden subject change. "I'm sorry."

Cecil pats Jack's hand and continues, "It was some kind of blood disorder or something. I don't really know. She would never talk to me about it." He sighs and gazes up at the branches again. "After she died, her consciousness came to me and told me she became a tree." It's as if he can sense Jack's next question, because he adds, "Consciousnesses are separate from physical forms, remember? They can still come to me even if they're already reincarnated."

Jack nods.

Cecil takes a deep breath and sighs. "I never knew which tree. Out of all the trees in the world, it's probably on another continent. You know, probability-wise? But sometimes I see one so breathtaking, so beautiful, that I think... maybe it's her."

"What was she like?" Jack asks.

Cecil smiles and says, "Everything you could want in a mother. Everything." Cecil looks over at him and pats his hand again, but lets it rest on top of Jack's. "Enough about my family. Let's talk to yours."

Cecil pulls a small notebook out of the pocket of his pants and a pen out of his jacket's. He opens it to a new page and starts scribbling in wide circles, then tight coils, then jagged zig zags.

"I'm getting— Oh my goodness." Immediately Cecil gets choked up and brings a hand to his face.

"Cecil?"

Cecil looks up at Jack with glistening eyes. He smiles at him and says through tears, "Jack Finch... you are so loved." He sniffles. "Mel has so much love for you. She's making that very clear to me." He continues drawing a spiral. "All that's coming through right now is just pure love."

Jack feels his throat tighten and wipes at his eyes quickly. Why would his father want to keep this from him?

Cecil doodles more and says, "I'm also seeing... She wants you to go on the tour— finish the tour. It will bring good into your life. She really wants you to go back out and finish it."

"Huh." Jack supposes she really was a big fan of his work. His family had told him how much she talked about the Ghost Checkers, even up until the end, but this proves how invested she was.

"A lot of good, Jack. It'll bring a lot of good into your life," Cecil says.

Jack nods and chews his cheek. He sighs and nudges some mulch around with his shoe.

"Can you tell her something?"

"She's right here with us, Jack. You can say it to her yourself."

Jack clears his throat. "Mel, I love you." He clears his throat again and leans his shoulders inward. The awkwardness of speaking out loud to something he can't see dissipates as he realizes he's really speaking to her again. Nothing else matters. "I've missed you every day. I keep expecting to see you every time I go into the living room. I keep hoping I'll wake up and that none of this would have ever happened." A sob wracks Jack, but he continues, "But you're gone, and I miss you, and I love you, and—and if you become someone else or something else I'll... I'll try and find you. Promise." Jack doesn't want to let go. Can't let go. He pauses and suddenly understands this is really it. This is final. "You try and find me too, okay?"

Jack has never cried in public and he hopes never to do so again, but for now, he couldn't care less. He rests his head in his hands as his shoulders shake and he releases every memory of her, dripping down his nose and onto the ground, watering the grass forcing its way up between bricks. With every gasping breath, he pours his love for her into the world, and maybe the air that carries it will find her, wherever she is.

A light pressure appears on Jack's upper back, Cecil resting a reassuring hand there. Jack sniffles and sits up.

"Thank you," he says to Cecil.

"My pleasure, Jack Finch."

They sit together on the bench for a long time before either of them breaks this fragile, grief-shaped silence.

Eventually, Cecil says, "Good news about the tour, huh?"

"Yeah," Jack says, an aching tone in his voice.

"I said the tour will be good for you. Why'd that make you sad?"

"I agree it would be good for me, but it's just not possible."

"Why?"

Jack looks over at him. "Because we can't go."

"But why?"

"Because we'd need you," Jack says, frustration growing in his voice.

"Okay?" Cecil says, still not understanding the problem.

"And I can't ask you to come back after what I did."

"Oh, honey," Cecil starts, tone gentle. "I forgave you days ago. Yeah, you kinda sucked for that, but hon, I'd be a fool to fault you. You perhaps could have phrased it a little kinder, but I understand." Cecil looks away. "You can't be friends with someone who diametrically opposes your worldview."

Jack insists, "We can be friends."

Cecil looks over at Jack and laughs. "Honey, it's okay. I understand."

"No, Cecil, you flew all the way to Florida for me. You contacted Mel for me. Why wouldn't I consider you a friend?"

"Because I'm a fraud, right?" Cecil bites out a bitter laugh.

Jack looks at him in disbelief. "Cecil, I don't think you're a fraud anymore. How could I? You gave me a way to talk to her one last time. Why would I still think that?"

It's Cecil's turn to tear up. "You really believe in me?"

Jack scoffs. "Uh, yeah. Pretty hard not to at this point. I don't know if you noticed, but I kinda just broke down on a public bench because of you."

They laugh, smiles sticking to their faces like the sap dripping down the oak tree's trunk. Cecil gazes up at its branches again and Jack wonders how he ever hated this man.

A couple weeks ago, all he saw in Cecil was a threat. But looking at him now, lights reflected in his eyes, casting a glow over his eyelashes, Jack wonders how he ever saw anything in this man but light.

All at once, Jack sees his future laid ahead of him like a vision. He sees joy and loss, but more than enough love to sustain him through it. He blinks, and when he opens his eyes, he sees Cecil, still sitting there, still gazing up at the tree.

Jack takes a breath, or maybe he lets one out, or maybe he stops needing to breathe all together, but he reaches his hand out to touch Cecil's shoulder, and when he looks over at him, Jack looks from his eyes to his lips. Cecil's eyes flick around Jack's face as if asking a question, but when he finds his answer this time, it's all Cecil needs before leaning up and kissing him.

Jack closes his eyes but still sees Christmas lights dancing behind his eyelids.

Cecil lifts his hands to Jack's shoulders, and Jack has never been so sure this is where he's meant to be.

They part, Cecil still looking into Jack's eyes with a question. Jack leans back down and pecks him on the lips again, silently answering him, *'yes, I mean it.'* Cecil smiles.

"Hello," Cecil breathes.

"Hi."

CHAPTER 16

A glow the color of Christmas lights has settled across Jack's vision even now, an hour after they returned home.

Jack is sitting on the couch watching Cecil get absolutely destroyed by Terri at dominoes. Every time Jack tries to stop smiling, a small grin finds its way back onto his face.

"Shoot," Cecil groans. "Guess I'll draw *again.*"

Terri puts down a domino and says, "Double five, everyone's gotta match it!"

"That is *not* how I played growing up," Cecil says. "All these crazy rules."

Only a couple hours ago, Jack was still hesitant about Cecil. Now it's as if a negative thought about him had never crossed his mind. Jack gazes at Cecil as he loses to Terri. Jack smiles.

Mel had been right all along. From the first rumor, she had known there would be something between them. He should have heard her out. It could have saved him so much angst.

But Jack supposes he needed to learn for himself that he could like Cecil, that he could accept him for who he is. Now that he has accepted him, he can move on to studying and understanding his gifts. Cecil is not frightening in the least, but the idea that psychics were real all along is. Luckily, understanding everything about them can solve that.

Cecil finishes putting the dominoes back in the tin and sits down next to Jack.

"Hello," he says as his knee bumps Jack's.

"Hi," Jack says, that persistent little smile returning to his face.

"Wanna go to your room?" Cecil whispers with a smile. Jack's face must morph into uncertainty because Cecil says, "Not for *that,* Jack Finch. Get your mind out of the gutter." Cecil stands and grabs Jack's hand to lead him down the hallway. Jack glances at Terri, who still has her back turned.

Cecil pulls Jack into his room and closes the door behind them. For a moment they just stand awkwardly in the middle of the room like teenagers about to have their first kiss. Cecil is the first to break the tension, stepping forward and wrapping his arms around Jack's neck.

"I missed you," Cecil says sweetly and leans up to kiss him.

"When?"

"When I was playing dominoes."

Jack pulls back and looks at him with a perplexed smile. "I was just in the living room."

"I know that. But I still missed you." Cecil kisses him again.

Jack sits down on the bottom bunk and Cecil walks closer. Jack reaches out for him. Cecil looks pretty thin, but Jack is pleased to find a softness at his waist. He reaches his left hand to touch Cecil's other side and pulls him closer.

Cecil lays his arms on Jack's shoulders, one hand tangling in his hair, his smile blooming.

"How are you feeling?" Jack asks.

"Pretty good," Cecil says.

"*Pretty* good?"

Cecil nods.

"Well, what can make it better?"

Cecil looks up and to the side, pretending to think for a moment before saying, "This." He leans down and kisses Jack on the nose.

Jack smiles at the way Cecil giggles and tugs him in closer, then turns so Cecil falls onto the bed. They stay that way for a while, Cecil laying on his back with his knees up, Jack's arms around him and head resting on his chest. Cecil runs his fingers through Jack's hair, and Jack has never felt more at home in his own skin.

"What's it like?" Jack asks. "Being psychic?"

Cecil chuckles, tangling his fingers in Jack's hair. "It's nice, sometimes. To be able to connect people to each other, like you and Mel. But most of the time"—Cecil's voice gains a tired edge—"it's hard. I don't usually see the future, but people's ancestors tell me what's in store for them constantly, good and bad, and it's a lot. It's hard." He pauses, then says, "It's isolating too, you know? People just not believing me constantly. Like you." Cecil ruffles his hair.

"I'm sorry it took me so long, Cecil."

"It's okay, sweetheart. I know I'm not the easiest to like, anyway."

Jack leans up on his elbows and looks at Cecil incredulously. "Not the—are you kidding? You're the easiest to like."

"You're sweet."

"No, I'm serious. You really grew on me," Jack says with a lopsided grin.

He settles his head back on Cecil's chest and his fingers play with the hem of his shirt.

"What's your favorite constellation?" Cecil asks a while later, his voice resonating in his chest under Jack's ear.

Jack shifts so he can look at Cecil, who is studying the glow-in-the-dark stars on the bottom of the top bunk that Jack put there when he was 13. "Constellation?" Jack repeats.

"Mm-hmm."

Jack thinks for a moment. He used to be interested in astronomy when he was younger. He and his father would go out late at night to look at the stars, or to try and catch a meteor shower. Mel would always relate it back to astrology and his father would promptly reject her assertions about the stars' effects on their emotions.

"I think it'd have to be Ursa Minor. Do you know that one?"

"It's the... wolf?"

"Bear. The small one." It was the first constellation Mel showed him how to find when he was little. "What about you?"

Cecil reaches a hand up and traces one of the larger stars. "You'll laugh at me."

Jack leans up on his elbows to look at him. He chuckles and says, "What are you talking about?"

"See? You're already laughing."

"No I'm not, see?" Jack makes a serious face and glares at him, and Cecil laughs even harder.

"Okay, fine. It's the little dipper," he says in a small voice.

"What?" Jack laughs. "Not even the big one?"

"I can never find the big one!"

"What do you mean?" Jack collapses onto him from laughter.

Cecil huffs, but can't help but laugh with him.

After Jack's laughter has faded into a smile, he says, "You know, the Little Dipper is actually made of some of the same stars as Ursa Minor."

"Really?"

"Yeah."

Cecil places his hands on either side of Jack's face and lifts his head to look at him. "So you're telling me... this whole time... we've been looking at the same stars?" Cecil says in a dramatic, cheesy voice.

"Oh, please," Jack laughs and drops his head back down onto Cecil's chest.

But they had been. Cecil, even though he was joking, was right. Both of their favorite constellations are interconnected, share the same stars, the same space in the sky.

If Jack were a man of symbolism, he'd probably think that means something.

A day later, Jack and Cecil are sitting at the dining table playing Uno when Jack's phone buzzes with a text from a number he doesn't recognize. He turns the screen face-down and continues playing.

Cecil smugly places a Draw Two card on the table, but Jack picks one of his own out of his hand and places it on top. Cecil groans and draws four.

Jack laughs, and it fades into a soft smile as he watches Cecil carefully arrange his newly-drawn cards in his hand. "So you said you never wanted to be a psychic."

Cecil hums in agreement and places a green seven down on the table.

Jack plays a green two and asks, "What *did* you want to be?"

Cecil smiles. "Before my path presented itself—" he begins, then cups his hand around his mouth like he's telling a secret and says, "or was chosen for me by my parents—I actually really wanted to be on TV."

"TV? Doing what?"

"Anything, honestly. I even daydreamed about being a weatherman for a while."

"A weatherman?" Jack finally draws another green card and plays it.

"A Draw Two? Really?" Cecil says, outraged, and draws his two cards. "But yes, a weatherman! I'd do a good job, don't ya think?" He sits up straighter and says, "And we have a cold weather system rolling in, so don't forget your umbrellas! Back to you, Susan."

Jack rubs his chin. "Hmm... I don't know."

"What, you don't think I'd have been good?"

"No, I think you'd be great." Jack smiles wryly. "But I think you'd distract from the forecast. You're too cute."

Cecil scoffs. "Oh, hush. Just for that, here—" He lays a Draw Two card of his own on the table.

Jack's phone buzzes again, and he ignores it.

"What did you want to be, Jackie my dear?"

Jack smiles. "At first, I wanted to be a bank robber."

"A bank robber? Ooh, sexy."

"You think?"

"For sure. On the run, heist after heist, bathing in piles of diamonds and bars of gold. Sexy."

"If you say so."

"So what'd you want to be after that?"

"Well, once I really got into the supernatural, I wanted to start my own consulting business," Jack says.

"Doing...?"

"House calls. Just helping people out."

"Well, isn't that kind of what you do already with the Ghost Checkers?"

Jack tilts his head back and forth and says, "Eh, not exactly. We aren't always doing house calls, you know. Plus, my way, there'd be no cameras."

"Why don't you do that, then?" Cecil asks.

"What do you mean?"

"I mean... go for it. Start it. How about... Finch Paranormal?"

"LLC," Jack adds.

"What?"

"LLC. Limited Liability Corporation. I'd have to add that for legal reasons."

"Okay, sure, whatever. But Finch Paranormal—don't you think that'd be a nice name?"

Jack thinks for a moment, pictures it. "Yeah. I think so."

"Well, then, you should do it. After the tour."

"I don't want to leave the group hanging, though."

"Okay, then, if—god forbid—you guys get cancelled," Cecil says. "Then you know you have a backup plan."

Jack nods. "If we get cancelled, yes." Jack plays a card. "But we won't get cancelled. We're gonna be fine."

"*You're* not!" Cecil says as he places down a blank wild card. "Draw 100!"

Jack laughs, but he's interrupted by his phone buzzing once again. "One second," he says to Cecil, turning his phone back over and looking at his notifications.

Unknown

Hi Jack

Did you know your phone number is available online

It was nice to see you yesterday

And at the meet and greet too

:)

Caty. She also attached a photo. Jack's blood goes cold and he drops his cards on the table.

"I can see your cards," Cecil teases, but he stops when he notices Jack's face.

Jack's hands shake as he enlarges the photo, clearly displaying Jack and Cecil kissing on the bench. "It's Caty."

"What'd she say?"

"She sent... a picture. Of us." Jack turns his phone so Cecil can see, and he gasps.

"That's so weird... Why was she there?"

Caty, their biggest, most intense fan was in Florida, states away from her home in Virginia, in the exact walking mall they were in. If it had been a coincidence, she would have freaked out and said hello. Instead, she hid behind them and secretly snapped photos.

She hid behind them and listened to him speak to his aunt for the last time. Jack pulls his cardigan tighter around himself.

She sends another text.

Unknown

I miss you

    Jack

    What do you want Caty

Unknown

Aw you knew it was me

I want to know why you cheated on me

Jack shows Cecil her text.

"Excuse me?" Cecil says.

Jack

I'm not your boyfriend

Unknown

Yes you are silly :)

You've been my boyfriend since we met

"This is so weird." Jack rubs a hand over his face.

Unknown

I hope you never cheat on me again

Or bye-bye Ghost Checkers :)

Jack reads her texts to Cecil, who gasps and says, "Who does she think she is?"

Jack

Are you threatening me?

Unknown

No baby of course not!

I love you too much to threaten you

But I will end your show

"I'm sorry, Cecil."

"No," Cecil says sharply, sticking a finger in the air. "You will *not* apologize for the actions of a crazed lunatic."

"What are we going to do?" Jack sighs.

"I don't know. Let's sit on it for a few days, okay? Maybe it will blow over, or we'll come up with a better idea."

Jack nods.

"Wanna play again?" Cecil says, gathering up the cards.

"Sure."

The next morning, Jack doesn't wake up to the smell of bacon. He realizes it's only 3 AM and tries to go back to sleep, but no matter how he lays, he isn't comfortable, and no matter where the blanket is, he's still too warm. Jack decides to get up for a while and try to go to sleep again a little later.

Jack steps out of his room, careful to avoid the creakiest floorboards, which he still somehow remembers. He walks into the kitchen to ransack the fridge, but sees he's already been beaten to it.

Cecil has the fridge door open, white light illuminating his bedhead and wrinkled tee. He glances over at Jack and nearly screams.

"Jack, you scared me half to death! I thought you were a ghost!"

Jack laughs and offers an apology, then walks to the pantry, placing a hand on Cecil's waist as he steps past him. He finds an open potato chip bag and unrolls it slowly, trying to avoid crinkling too much.

Jack takes a seat on a barstool and offers the bag to Cecil, who sits down next to him and takes a small handful.

"Why can't you sleep?" Jack asks him.

Cecil rests his head on Jack's shoulder. "Dreams."

"Nightmares?"

"Pretty much. For the last few weeks I've been dreaming about this face. I don't know whose it is. It's just scary."

"I bet. Sorry you've been having those." Jack thinks for a moment, munching on a chip. They're pretty stale, but he's hungry. "The last few weeks? So during the tour?"

"Yeah. That's why I kept falling asleep all the time. Those dreams just have a way of keeping me up at night."

Jack nods his head.

After a few minutes, Jack can feel that quiet pull of sleep and doesn't want to miss his opportunity, so he says goodnight to Cecil with a kiss and heads back to bed.

As Jack closes his eyes, he can't help but think about Cecil and his nightmares. Jack had his fair share of nightmares as a kid. Mel was the best at calming him down afterwards.

Jack hears floorboards creak as Cecil goes back to bed, and Jack sits up. He quietly makes his way to the guest room and knocks quietly.

"Jack?" he hears from inside.

Jack opens the door slowly and peeks in. "Can I come in here?"

Cecil is sitting up in bed, about to get comfortable. "Of course, sweetheart. What's wrong?"

"I just wanted to be here for you. Nightmares suck."

Cecil chuckles. "They do."

Jack rounds the bed and lifts the covers, slipping in behind Cecil. He wraps his arm around him and rests the bridge of his nose against the nape of Cecil's neck.

"Good night."

"Good night, Jack Finch," Cecil says sleepily.

The next time Jack wakes up, late morning sunlight is streaming in through the lacey curtains, casting a glow on the cross stitch geese. The bed is empty save for himself. He sits up and stretches, then heads to his own room, pulls on a shirt, and walks out into the living room.

Again, there is no bacon scent in the air. He looks around and there is no sign of Cecil.

Terri is sipping coffee at the breakfast bar.

"You seen Cecil?" Jack asks her, but she shakes her head.

Jack wanders back down the hallway to the bathroom and listens quietly at the door. He realizes he's being creepy and is about to leave when he hears Cecil speaking quietly, presumably on the phone.

"—just don't know if it's a good idea... I know, and I'll ask him, I just... Yeah... I'm glad you understand... I'll let you know later today."

Jack jumps out of the way just in time to miss getting hit by the door.

"Jack! Jeez Louise, you scared me. What are you doing there?"

"I was just coming to check on you."

"Oh, well aren't you sweet? I'm right as rain, my dear."

"Did I hear you on the phone?" Jack asks, trying to give him the opportunity to talk about it.

Instead, Cecil says, "Oh, it wasn't anything. It was the airline trying to get me to take a survey." Cecil walks past him and into the living room. Jack frowns.

He feels a buzz in his pocket and looks at his phone. It's a text from Lydia: *'is this too much?'* with a link to a tweet.

The tweet is from Lydia and Adeel's fake Twitter, Bianca. It says, *'i just spotted lydia clarke-west and adeel sahni absolutely MAKING OUT please retweet this.'*

Jack texts back, *'Not at all. Personally, I think it's a little subtle.'*

At lunch, Cecil and Terri chat happily while the rest of them listen, eating their sandwiches. Jack is glad not to have to make conversation. He likes all these people, obviously, but he's not much of a conversationalist.

"So, Cecil, honey. When is your return flight?" Terri asks him.

Cecil gives Jack an odd look so quickly Jack almost misses it. "Not sure. I like to book them at the last minute. You can get great deals that way, you know."

"Is that true?" Terri asks him and they proceed to discuss the best travel hacks Cecil knows.

After lunch, Cecil offers to do dishes, so Jack picks up Terri's plate and his own and follows him in.

Once in the privacy of the kitchen, Jack corners Cecil by the dishwasher and says, "What's going on?"

Cecil laughs brightly and says, "What do you mean?"

"I heard you on the phone this morning. It wasn't the airline. Who were you talking to?"

"I—nobody. Jack, get out of my way please."

Jack steps aside and says, "I deserve to know." In a softer voice, he adds, "Don't I?"

Cecil turns back around. "Oh, sweetie, of course you do. I just—" he sighs. "It was Austin on the phone. He wants to continue the tour but—"

"But you don't want to." Jack looks down at his feet and notices there is a hole forming in his sock above his big toe.

"No, no!" Cecil says, waving his hands. "I just don't know if it's what's best for you."

"For me?"

Cecil steps forward and gently holds Jack's forearms. "Yes, Jack. You just lost someone very important to you. You need time to grieve. I'm not sure a haunted house is the best place to do that."

Jack leans back against the counter and considers this. No, it's not conventional, but is any of this really conventional? Jack thinks about what Terri told him: that Mel had been so excited for his tour and talked about it until the end. Through Cecil, Mel said it herself: that she wants him to finish the tour. That it would be good for him. No, a haunted house is not a normal place to grieve, and it might be a poor choice were it anyone else, but this is Mel. In all honesty, this might be the best possible way to honor her. "I want to go."

"What? Jack, I—"

"You said it yourself last night. Mel thinks it will bring good things into my life. She wants me to go. Why shouldn't I listen?"

Cecil eyes him. "If you're sure…"

"I am."

"Okay." Cecil sighs and pulls out his phone, sending a text.

Jack's phone buzzes a few seconds later; it's the group chat.

Austin

WELCOME BACK JACKIE

Lydia

WOOHOO

Ferris

AAAAAAAAAAAA

Adeel

Yay

A few seconds later, Adeel texts again:

Adeel

Lydia says that seems sarcastic but it's not

I'm happy :)

Jack could cry. He misses these people so much. He's glad he could come back to be with his family this week, but he's aching to see his other family again too.

"Austin says to meet them in Maryland. Apparently, we can still make the last stop," Cecil says.

"The last stop? That's the Amerigo house," Jack realizes, and his persistent smile returns.

Telling his father goes as well as he can hope. Jack is sitting on the porch beside him, both swaying gently in their rocking chairs.

"You know what I think about that show of yours."

"I know."

"And you know your aunt's funeral is in two days."

"I know."

"And you know I was expecting you to deliver a eulogy for her."

"I... did not know that."

"Hm. Maybe I told Terri. Point is, you know what I think about you ditching your family to go have fun."

"But dad," Jack starts, "it's not just fun. It's my job. And it's people I care about. Not that I don't care about the people here because I obviously do, but I—"

"You know what I think, Jack, but here's what I'll say: you're an adult. Do what you think is best."

Great. The 'what you think is best' card, the ultimate parental manipulation tool. Fun. Makes Jack feel great.

Jack watches a blue jay as it lands on the birdbath. Cicadas screech away in the tree to Jack's right. His skin starts to feel sticky from the humidity and he settles further back into his rocking chair. A mosquito whines in his ear and he bats it away. "I'm gonna go," he says. "They need me. Mel wanted me to go, and it's important for my career."

"What do you mean Mel wanted you to go?"

"She told me."

"When?"

"Yester…"–Oh. His dad doesn't know why Cecil was here. Too late to lie, word already halfway out of mouth– "…day. Cecil's a psychic. He contacted her."

"What have I always said? There is never a reason to contact a spirit."

"I know, but dad, I had a reason. I wanted to talk to her again."

His dad levels a heavy gaze on him. "Jack, I always told you to be careful–"

"I know, but dad, I had to talk to her. It wasn't like you. I didn't get sucked in."

Wrong thing to say. His father's gaze hardens and he looks away, rocking slowly in his chair.

"Dad, I'm sorry, you know I didn't mean it like that—"

"How do you know this kid isn't just making it all up? A lot of people who say they're psychic aren't worth shit."

"Well, I kind of think he might be... worth shit. He convinced me."

"Then I'm sorry I raised my son to be so gullible."

Jack gapes at him, then looks away. He watches a blackbird hopping around in the grass.

"I'm gonna go, dad," Jack says quietly. "To Maryland."

"I sincerely hope it is everything you want it to be."

Jack stands and looks at his father, who keeps staring straight ahead. "Thanks." Jack goes back inside and hopes he never turns into him.

CHAPTER 17

Cecil was right about booking flights last minute because in a matter of hours he has them booked on flight 538 with nonstop service from Orlando to Baltimore. The night before their flight, Jack is staring up at the sagging cross boards of the upper bunk, gently illuminated by the green glaze of the glow-in-the-dark stars.

He glances at his phone: 3:48 AM. They need to be at the airport in three hours to comfortably make their 9 AM flight. They hadn't discussed when they'd leave. Jack bets Cecil is one of those reckless types who arrives at the airport thirty minutes before their boarding time. He shudders and hopes that's not the case.

Jack sleeps for an hour or so more before turning over and realizing he's wide awake. He glances at his phone again and sees that he beat his alarm by four minutes. Nice.

Jack throws his legs over the edge of the bed and sits up, yawning. His shoulder cramps when he stretches a bit too hard. Getting older is fun.

He felt so young at the beginning of all this Ghost Checkers stuff in 2016 when it was just Austin and him. The two of them would go from cemetery to cemetery, abandoned building to abandoned building with just a shaky camcorder and Jack's dad's EMF meter. In those days, Jack and Austin would stay up all night editing videos and going through hours of footage and recordings, powered only by Redbull and Doritos. They eventually saved up enough from their YouTube ad revenue to buy better equipment, and that's when their views picked up and they gained the attention of Funbuzz. That's when everything changed.

It changed generally for the better. He met Lydia, Ferris, and Adeel, and their budget (and pay) increased exponentially. But some part of him misses the days when he and Austin just lived ad paycheck to ad paycheck, booking cheap motels or crashing in Austin's mom's van. It wasn't glamorous, but it was a life they carved out for themselves.

It was during these days that Jack met Caty. Oh, Caty, with her unsettling smile and eyes that always open a little too wide. She loved them, and at first, they loved her. Their first superfan. How cool is that?

But she got more and more intense, leaving graphic comments, showing up at restaurants they hadn't told anyone they were going to, leaving them letters in their mailboxes.

She finally settled down after a couple years and they hadn't heard from her again until the meet and greet, and now those texts. Jack rereads her messages. Is there any way these could be read that *don't* suggest a threat? Jack doesn't think so.

He sighs and tosses his phone back onto the bed, scrubbing his hands over his face. There's no way he's giving up on Cecil. This will blow over. It has to.

"Cecil, we're gonna be late," Jack says outside the bathroom, drumming his fingers on his thigh. When he gets no answer, he says, "Cecil?" and tries the handle.

The door slowly swings open and when he hears no scandalized objection, Jack peers in. He sees Cecil leaning over the sink.

"Hi," Cecil says and huffs out a laugh. "Dropped my contact."

"Oh. Do you... You don't have an extra?"

"Nope," Cecil says with a pop on the 'p'.

"So what do we... do?"

Cecil sighs. "Ugh, guess I'll wear"—Cecil closes his eyes and shudders—"my glasses."

"Oh. And you have those with you?"

"I do." Cecil sighs. "They're always in my bag in case of situations like this, but Jack, they aren't very... flattering, I suppose you could say."

Flattering? Why does that matter when they're about to miss their flight?

Cecil walks past him and towards the guest bedroom and Jack follows. Cecil rummages around in a zipper pocket of his duffel bag and pulls out a large hard-shell glasses case. He glances at Jack, then turns away from him and puts them on. When he turns back around, Jack can barely stop a laugh from bubbling out of his throat.

Cecil was right: they're not flattering. They are bright red and huge on him, taking up half his face, and the lenses must be strong because they magnify his eyes comically large. He thought his 'type' included glasses, but now he's not so sure. "You look like a bug."

Cecil gasps indignantly. "A bug, Mr. Finch? Well, I could say a few things about you, too, if ya wanna hear 'em."

Jack laughs and holds up a placating hand. "No, that's okay. I was just kidding. You look—good." Jack's voice breaks and he snorts. "Like a cute bug."

Cecil's eyes go wide at that and he laughs at him, his glasses slipping partway down his nose. Without thinking, Jack reaches up and fixes them.

"Oh," Cecil breathes. "Thank you."

"No problem," Jack answers, barely above a whisper. He reaches up again and brushes a bouncy curl behind Cecil's ear, and like magnets, their lips find each other again.

After several moments, Jack remembers himself and grunts out, "Mm!" and pulls back. "We need to go. Like, now."

"Right! Yes. Okay. Let me find my shoes."

After several minutes of looking, he finally finds them ("They were by the front door where I left them!") and they head out.

The Orlando airport is never a pleasant experience. The TSA officers are as rude as ever, the lines are disgustingly long, and the whole place smells a little bit like an old bagel. But this is different from every time Jack has walked through the high-ceilinged halls, because now he has Cecil by his side. Jack glances down at him and fights the urge to lay an arm over his shoulder. It could jeopardize the team if it somehow got back to Caty that they're still dating.

Dating. Are they dating? Jack thinks back over the last few days. They kissed (a lot), but they never really spoke about what they are.

Jack glances down at Cecil again, now trying to text and navigate throngs of people simultaneously. Cecil glances up and narrowly avoids a luggage cart.

Jack thinks he might like to date him. Like, really date him. When he wasn't wasting time glaring at him, Jack really has enjoyed Cecil's company the last couple weeks. He's funny and smart and considerate, and probably everything

Jack would look for in a guy. The psychic stuff is pretty far out of Jack's comfort zone, already making him question the world around him, but maybe that's a good thing.

The pair arrives at gate 44 and Cecil confirms on their boarding passes that it's the right one. Jack glances around. There are several sections of seating with many people in various states of slumber. One old man has his arms crossed and his chin to his chest. He starts drifting to his right and startles himself awake. One woman has claimed a full row of seats, laying with her head pillowed on her balled-up coat, her bags taking up the rest of the row. Another woman sits on the floor so she can charge her phone. Jack shudders to think what's crawling around in the airport carpets.

Jack and Cecil sit side by side in a mostly empty block of seats. Cecil tosses his duffel bag into the seat beside him, and Jack balances his backpack on top of his suitcase. Immediately Cecil pulls out his phone and Jack smirks.

Around a quarter past seven, Jack's stomach starts rumbling.

"Hey, if I go get something to eat, are you good to watch our bags here?"

"Mm-hmm," Cecil says without looking up.

"Do you want anything?"

Cecil glances at him and smiles. "Aren't you a sweetheart? No, I'm good for now, hon."

Jack walks through airport retail hell. He passes a sit-down Italian restaurant, two luggage boutiques, a kiosk selling perfumes, magnets, and teddy bears, and a Disney store before reaching a regular old magazines-and-candy type of airport shop.

Tabloids, puzzle books, and Nicholas Sparks novels line the walls with a circular snack-lined checkout desk in the center. Jack peruses their snack selection and ends up getting strawberry Starbursts, a bag of pizza-flavored Combos, and, what the heck—he throws a Nicholas Sparks book on the counter too. He finished his alien romance and needs something to read on the plane anyway.

The teenage girl at the counter who looks way too cool to be working here rings him up. He thanks her, takes his bag, and heads back into the nightmare of the Orlando airport. Something wafts beneath his nose and, no—though he's in Florida, for once it is not the smell of pee. He turns and sees a pretzel kiosk.

Jack wonders if Cecil likes pretzels. He seems like a pretzel kind of guy, so he waits in the short line and grabs one for him.

When he returns to the gate, he hands it to Cecil.

"Oh, thank you."

Jack cocks his head at the lack of a pet name. Since they kissed the first time, Cecil is always calling him 'honey' or 'sugar', or something else along those lines.

Jack glances up and sees three teen girls gawking at him.

"Oh my god, it's Jack Finch!"

Jack's eyes widen and he feels his face go white.

"Oh my gosh, Mr. Finch, I have loved your videos for*ever*," one girl says.

"We love Lydia too but OMG you're the best one."

The other girls nod.

"Is Adeel nice in person?"

Jack blinks and sits down. "The nicest."

"And what about Lydia? Is she really that crazy?"

Jack laughs. "Most of the time. You'd be surprised though. She has a serious side. One time, we were investigating this B&B in Vermont and while we were there, someone tried breaking in. I don't think we were able to post that video because of legal reasons since there was an ongoing investigation around it, but man, you should have seen her. I've never seen someone give a robber such a piece of their mind like that before." Jack realizes the girls are hanging on every word and smiles. Yes, he likes anonymity, but he doesn't mind it when people like him, too.

"Girls," a woman a few rows away calls.

"Oh, we have to go. But thank you. Um... Could we have a picture really quick?"

"Sure," Jack agrees, and reaches his hand to take her phone but she looks confused. "Oh, of us?"

"Yeah," she says, nodding her head.

"Okay." Jack doesn't remember anyone ever asking to take a picture with just him, especially when there is another member of the team right next to him.

"I'll take it," Cecil offers. They all stand and Cecil snaps a few pictures.

"Thank you," one of the girls says nervously. "Bye."

Jack waves goodbye and sits back down. "That was crazy."

"You've never been recognized before?"

"Not like that, not out of context. No one has ever been that happy to see me."

"Beg to differ, Jack Finch."

"What, you?" Jack says, a smile creeping up on him.

"Is it a crime to be happy to see your b—" Cecil stops. "Best bud?" he says instead.

Was he about to say 'boyfriend'? They never had a frank conversation about what they are to each other, but Jack is still surprised to find out Cecil would be that serious about him. Maybe it was just a genuine slip of the tongue. Who knows?

Cecil scrolls on his phone while Jack begins his novel. It's called *Every Breath*. The main character's name is Hope and the love interest's name is Tru. Jack rolls his eyes. It's about two strangers who fall in love, but have to decide if they're more loyal to their family or their new love. It sounds dreadful, and Jack is intrigued. Cecil runs to the bathroom and Jack promises to watch his duffel bag.

A few minutes into reading, a shadow falls across the page and Jack looks up. In front of him stands a teen boy and a woman who looks to be his mother.

"Hello," Jack says tentatively.

"Hi," the woman says. "This is my son, Hunter. He thinks he recognizes you."

"Are you Jack Finch?"

Jack dog ears the page he's on and closes his book. "Yes, I am,"

"I really like—"

"He really likes your internet videos," the woman says, her hands on her son's shoulders.

He shrugs her off. "Mom," he whines.

"He was wondering if he could get a photo."

"Mom, I can talk!" Hunter says, exasperated. "...Yeah, can I get a photo?"

"Sure," Jack says, an amused smile on his face.

Hunter sits down in Cecil's empty seat and they lean closer together as Hunter's mom snaps a photo.

"You know, Cecil will be back soon if you want a picture with him."

"Who?"

"Come on, Hunter," his mom says. "Let's get back to our seats. Thank you," she says through a toothy smile.

"No problem." Jack smiles at both of them and they return to their seats. He was recognized by himself, not even in the context of his teammates. This kid didn't even know who Cecil was. Jack doesn't expect the small swell of pride he feels in his chest.

"Did I see you takin' another photo?" Cecil asks as he walks back to his seat, a smile in his voice.

"Yep. He recognized me."

"Well, look at you, Mr. Celebrity!"

"I don't know about that."

"What do you mean?" Cecil cocks his head at Jack.

"Well, I don't know." Jack smooths his hands down the thighs of his jeans. "I mean, it's just a YouTube show and I'm not even the fan favorite."

"You are *too* the fan favorite!"

"Not really, no. Everybody prefers Lydia. And now you, too."

"Jack." Cecil looks at him sternly. "Have you not even looked at the forums?"

"Forums?"

"Oh, you are hopeless." Cecil pulls out his phone again and opens Reddit. He searches 'Ghost Checkers' and taps on the forum that pops up, then he taps the first post. "Look." Cecil holds his phone where Jack can see.

The original post in the thread says *Petition for Jack to get more screen time.* Cecil scrolls through a few of the comments, all agreeing with the original poster. He goes on to another post, which is just screenshots of recent episodes zoomed in on Jack's arms.

"Why'd they post that?" Jack asks as he squints at the photos of his biceps.

"Uh... I don't know, maybe because *you're hot?*" Cecil answers. "Jack, come on. Your fans freaking love you. I am right in calling you 'Mr. Celebrity'."

Jack looks at him skeptically.

"Back at the meet and greet, like 200 people were excited to see *you*, and today, two groups of people recognized you in a random airport in the last, like, twenty minutes."

"I guess that's true... Well, one group recognized you first."

"Yeah, because I'm also Mr. Celebrity."

"We have the same last name?" Jack asks.

"Yes. You took my last name in this scenario."

"Oh, so we're married?"

"Clearly."

"Well, I would have preferred we hyphenated."

"Noted."

Jack smiles, amusedly. "Noted?"

"Yes, for when we inevitably get married and become America's favorite couple. *Someone* has to fill the Brangelina-shaped hole left in the American zeitgeist."

"And you think that couple will be us?"

"Jack," Cecil starts, "look at us. The country's favorite ghost hunter and the world's favorite psychic? Please."

"How come I'm the country's favorite but you're the world's favorite?"

"You still have a lot you can learn from me, my sweet Jack. I am the original Mr. Celebrity, after all." Cecil cups Jack's cheek, then pinches it like a grandma.

Cecil pops his earbuds in, curls up in his chair, and rests his head on his neck pillow. He's out in thirty seconds.

Jack reads for a while longer.

Then he feels someone tap him on the shoulder.

He looks up and sees a wide smile that feels like spiders crawling on his skin. *Caty.*

"Hey, sweetheart!" she says and sits down on his other side.

"What are you doing here?"

"Checking on you."

Jack crosses his arms and leans away from her. "Why?"

Caty glances at Cecil, still sleeping soundly. "I just wanted to make sure you remember our texts. It's embarrassing, honestly,"—she reaches up and softly trails a finger down Jack's cheek—"when the whole world thinks your boyfriend is dating someone else."

Jack slaps her hand away. "I'm not your boyfriend."

Caty smiles at him. "One day, though." She reaches for his hand and he jerks away, elbowing Cecil by accident.

Cecil stirs awake and takes an earbud out. He spots Caty and gasps. "You! What are you doing here?"

Caty sneers at him and doesn't answer. Instead, she says, "You look tired. You should go back to sleep."

Cecil gasps and takes out his other earbud. "Caitlyn Ann Peterson, do you even have a flight?"

"How do you know my name?"

"I'm psychic, bitch. If you don't have a flight, you're not supposed to be at the gate."

"Well, I do have a flight."

"Oh, do you?"

"Yes, I'm going back to Virginia. I had a lovely vacation in Florida, but it's time to go home." She looks at Jack and smiles. "I got some lovely pictures, though. Are you two going back to meet the team?"

Jack nods, eyes firmly on the mottled carpet.

"Aw. Well enjoy it," Caty says dangerously.

"Oh, would you shut up?" Cecil says. "Better get to your gate or you'll miss your flight."

Caty laughs. "You don't even know what flight I'm on."

A woman comes on over the loudspeaker and announces a flight to Virginia is now boarding.

Cecil points upwards and says, "Is it that one?"

Caty glares at him, then smiles at Jack. Her face changes so quickly, eyes becoming full of some kind of twisted love, that Jack has to stifle a shudder. "See you soon, sweetheart." She grabs at his hand so he pulls away again, and Caty laughs.

Jack shrinks in his chair as Cecil keeps his eyes on Caty, glaring at her until she's out of sight.

As soon as he's done watching her, Cecil grabs Jack's hand and says, "Oh my god, that was awful. What the hell? Why does she think she can just—just—menace you like that? And what she said about 'enjoying' going back to the team. That sounded like a threat. Are you okay?"

Jack turns his hand over under Cecil's and squeezes. "I'm fine. That was just..." Jack wipes his other hand on his knee. "Weird."

"So weird." Cecil leans his head on Jack's shoulder. "I'm sorry about her," he mumbles into Jack's cardigan. "Do you need anything?"

"A Xanax," Jack jokes.

"Oh, I have those. I told my doctor I have flight anxiety."

"Do you?"

"No. Want one?"

Jack laughs and shakes his head. He had forgotten how adept Caty is at stalking, and how nerve-racking it is to have her pop up randomly. It's never random though.

A woman announces that their flight is now boarding. A few minutes later, she calls their zone and they gather their bags and get in line.

Jack stares out the large window to his left at the plane waiting for them. The sun has already risen on the other side of the sky but still throws a glow of orange onto the clouds on Jack's side of the horizon.

They scan their boarding passes and step onto the plane. Cecil takes the window seat and Jack sits in the middle. Now's not a bad time to pull out some Ferris advice. Jack chants to himself: *'Normal person, normal person, normal person.'*

Thankfully a very regular-seeming middle-aged woman sits beside him and doesn't say a word after, "Hello."

They watch the safety demonstration, then stare out the window for thirty minutes as the plane drives around ("I wonder if they ever do donuts?"), before the captain finally announces takeoff. The plane gets into position, then they lift into the air.

Not long after that, Cecil is snoring on Jack's shoulder.

After watching Florida fall away until the sights of the swamps below are replaced with clouds, Jack opens his book and begins reading.

He gets about forty pages in before Cecil stirs beside him. Jack looks over and sees him looking up at Jack with a sweet smile, head still pillowed on his shoulder. "Hi."

"Hello," Cecil says, smiling even bigger.

Jack closes his book. "Good nap?"

"The best." Cecil stretches as much as the cramped window seat will allow. (At his height, he has significantly more legroom than Jack, though.) Cecil rests his head back on Jack's shoulder, then cups his hand on Jack's cheek and pulls him down for a kiss.

"Cecil," Jack whispers. "Someone could see." Jack wants to glance around the cabin to try and spot Caty, part of him certain she got on their flight, but he keeps his eyes fixed on Cecil.

Cecil leans up again, their kiss chaste and lingering. "Who saw?"

Jack glances around and expects to see that spine-tingling grin, but he only makes eye contact with the woman beside him. She smiles and winks, then pointedly looks away.

Cecil yanks him back down again. When they part, Cecil is the first to start giggling.

Jack shushes him, but his laughter is contagious, and he can't help but giggle too. So there they are, two adults giggling like teens about kissing on an airplane. This is what Jack's life has become. He doesn't mind very much.

The pilot comes over the speakers and announces their final descent and Jack glances out the window. Cecil is sleeping again, so Jack taps him and points to the glowing city centers drifting below them.

"Beautiful," Cecil breathes.

"Yeah," Jack agrees.

"We should go on a trip one day, just you and me," Cecil says.

"Really? You'd want to do that?"

"Of course. What about... California? A couple months from now?"

Jack can picture it, just the two of them exploring a city together, and his stomach flutters. "Okay... But what about the paparazzi?"

"Paparazzi?"

"Yeah. America's favorite couple? We're sure to be swamped."

"Oh, very true, very true. Mm-hmm. Well, I suppose we could wear disguises."

"Yeah?"

"Yeah." Cecil looks at him and studies his face. He takes off his glasses and puts them on Jack. Then he holds up a finger and lays it across Jack's upper lip. "A mustache and glasses would do you well."

"Really? I think... full prosthetics for you."

Cecil laughs. "What? Why?"

"Because you're so handsome. Anything less than a complete facial change and you'd be recognized for sure."

Cecil laughs and smacks Jack's shoulder. "Hush, you."

The plane lands and not long afterwards the seatbelt light dings off, and everyone scrambles up and out of their seats, pulling their bags out of the overhead compartments in a frenzy.

Cecil and Jack worm their way off the plane and find themselves in the Baltimore airport.

"Bathroom!" Cecil exclaims, hanging his duffel back on Jack's shoulder and running into the restroom. Jack chuckles and stands outside the bathroom to wait for him. He takes this time to check his phone.

Austin

Looking forward to seeing you guys

Lydia

srsly so excited

Ferris

its not the same without u :(

Adeel

I hope your flight goes really well :)

　　Jack

　　Thanks guys. Off flight. Be out soon.

Cecil emerges from the restroom, flapping his hands in the air. Jack gives him a look.

"What? There weren't paper towels, just those air thingies I hate."

Jack laughs and hands Cecil's duffel bag back to him and they head to baggage claim. Jack has far less trouble getting his bag this time, mainly thanks to Cecil and the closure Jack was able to find.

They step onto the escalators, fingers interlaced, hidden behind the person in front of them, and Jack feels more at peace than he has these last few weeks.

Then he spots them: his favorite people. Ferris and Lydia are jumping up and down, Adeel is waving sweetly, and Austin is holding a sign: *Mr. Jack Finch.* Jack smiles.

They reach the bottom of the escalator and their friends rush over to them.

"Welcome back!" Ferris shouts.

Ferris and Adeel each give them hugs, then pick up their bags and head to the minivan waiting beyond the automatic doors. Austin hands his sign to Lydia and wraps Jack in a tight hug.

"I love you, and I'm happy you're here," he whispers.

Jack breathes shakily and hugs Austin tighter.

When they let go, Jack turns and sees Cecil and Lydia pulling back from a hug.

"Nice glasses," she teases. "You look like Chicken Little."

"Nice hair," Cecil replies. "You look like... McDonald's French fries."

Lydia laughs and looks offended. "Jack, did you hear that?" she asks as they all climb back into the van.

"Yep."

"Aren't you going to disagree?"

"Nope."

CHAPTER 18

"So..." Austin drums his hands on the steering wheel. "Why were you guys traveling together anyway?" There is a subtle edge to his voice that Jack doesn't like.

"Cecil actually came to visit me in Florida," Jack answers.

"Is that so?" Austin says, glancing at Cecil in the rearview mirror.

"Yeah. He, uh... He spoke to Mel for me."

"What?" Ferris says, confused. "Like... *spoke to her, spoke to her*? Like, psychicly?"

"Yeah," Jack confirms.

"And that's... okay with you?" Lydia asks.

Jack laughs. "Guys, yes. I accept things that are true. I know it's true now. I'm actually looking forward to studying it more now that I know I can."

"That's great, Jack," Austin says with a smile. "Did... anything *else* happen?"

Jack frowns. "What are you getting at?"

Austin glances over. "We—Okay, well, we kind of had a bet—"

"About when you and Cecil were gonna get together," Lydia interrupts. She starts counting on her fingers. "Austin said last week, I said in the airport, and Ferris said it'll happen after you get back."

"What about Adeel?" Cecil asks.

"I didn't participate, you guys. I respect you too much," Adeel explains.

"So...?" Austin starts. "When did it happen?"

Jack is at a loss for words, but Cecil jumps in. "Y'all are too much, seriously," he laughs. "Nothing happened on our trip. We're not together, you guys. And we're not going to get together."

Lydia groans. "Does this mean we owe Adeel money? He's the only one that wasn't wrong."

"I don't know how bets work," Ferris admits. "Like, at all."

"How about we all keep our fifty dollars and call it a draw?" Austin suggests.

"Fifty bucks?" Jack repeats. "That's a lot."

"Yeah," Cecil agrees. "Is it too late for me to bet?"

"Mel really said that?" Lydia asks Cecil. The team is laying around the extra hotel room Austin booked when he found out Jack and Cecil were coming back.

"Clear as day," Cecil says. "She told me Jack would get a lot of good out of this tour."

"So you heard her voice?" Adeel asks.

Cecil scrunches his mouth and thinks. "I heard her, felt her. It's all part of a knowingness that comes over me, a sensation in my body, an image they project, words they speak. I've learned to add it all up and interpret what they mean."

"That's so cool how you've just figured that all out. Is that what your book is going to be about?"

Oh yeah, Cecil's book, the whole reason he came on their tour in the first place.

"Sort of? I guess—well, honestly, I'm still not sure what it's even gonna be about, really. A collection of anecdotes, a how-to, a guide to the afterlife… I really don't know."

"Do you feel like you're any closer to figuring it out?" Austin asks.

"Of course!" Cecil wraps his arms around Ferris and Lydia who sit on either side of him. "And I'm sure by the end of this whole thing I'll know exactly what I want to write about." Cecil glances at Jack, and he really hopes that look doesn't mean Cecil is including him in the book. Jack is a private sort of person and being included in a book spectacularizing his field of study is not exactly something he wants. Sure, he likes Cecil now, and sure, he understands there is more to learn about the world, but Cecil, psychic or not, is still a showman, and his book will undoubtedly reflect that.

"Well," Austin says, patting the arm of his chair and standing. "We oughta edit the rest of the footage." He says to Jack, "We've been working on finishing up the rest of the episodes while you guys were gone. We only have— Ferris, one or two more?"

"Two more."

"Two more," Austin repeats to Jack, who nods, impressed.

"Nice."

"Alrighty, Ferris, Adeel, McDonald's fries, come with me."

Lydia glares at Cecil and says, "You did this." Then she laughs and the four of them leave the room, heading upstairs to the other hotel room. Since Austin added on this room later, they weren't able to book them near each other like usual, so they have a ways to go.

The door shuts and Cecil stands up. "Just you and me," he says, walking towards Jack, "in this big ole room."

Jack chuckles. "Whatever shall we do?"

"I have an idea," Cecil says as he sits across Jack's lap on the small sofa. Jack smiles into their kiss and brings his hands up to Cecil's waist, hitching up his button up and feeling the soft skin there.

"Why are you smiling?" Cecil asks between kisses.

"Because you're you," Jack replies, "and I like you."

Their lips come together again like the sun touching the horizon, and the bright colors of their sunset swim behind Jack's eyelids. They continue like this, catching quick breaths between kisses, eagerly enjoying their alone time until the door unlocks and clicks open.

"Sorry, forgot my—*oh.*"

Jack and Cecil both snap their heads to see Ferris standing shocked in the doorway.

"Ferris—" Jack starts.

Ferris breaks into a smile and starts slowly backing out of the room. "You got together... I won the bet," they whisper before they take off running, Jack and Cecil in hot pursuit.

If Ferris tells the team, Lydia will tell all of Twitter (through no fault of her own—the whole team knows she can't keep a secret), which would anger Caty and endanger the whole group.

"Ferris, stop!" Jack says in a hushed voice, not wanting to yell in a public place. Ferris darts around a corner and when Jack and Cecil catch up to them, they're in the elevator with the doors closing.

"Stairs!" Cecil says, breathing heavily.

"Good idea." The two dart up the next two flights of stairs, Jack's thighs burning. He bursts through the door and onto the 6th floor just as the elevator doors ding open. Ferris steps out and upon seeing them, runs down the hallway.

Cecil, apparently having gotten his second wind, darts after them. Jack, who has not gotten his second wind, jogs behind the pair. Ferris struggles to swipe their keycard and Cecil catches up and tackles them, but not before the door opens. They both fall forward into the room as Ferris chokes out, "Cecil and Jack just got together!" The two of them hit the floor with a *thud* and Ferris says weakly, "I win."

Jack catches up to them and stands in the doorway, looking at the pile of person in front of him. He slowly looks up at Lydia, Austin, and Adeel sitting on one of the beds. They're all making the same expression: eyes wide, jaws on the floor.

Jack smiles halfheartedly. "Surprise?"

"Okay, so tell me again. What happened on the bench?" Lydia says eagerly, practically swooning.

"Jack swept me off my feet and kissed me like Prince Charming."

"Not exactly," Jack says. "We were just sitting on a bench. I think it had bird poop all over it."

"It was magical," Cecil sighs.

"So I don't win?" Ferris mutters.

"That's amazing!" Lydia exclaims. "My two sweet boys, together forever." She hugs both of them tightly around the neck. Jack taps her elbow and when she lets go, he sucks in a breath. "My boys," she says, pretending to be tearful. "All grown up." Lydia pinches Jack's cheek.

"Lay off of 'em," Austin says, smiling from the kitchenette. The microwave beeps and he pulls out his popcorn. As he walks over, he says, "So why weren't you gonna tell us?"

Jack scrubs a hand over his cheek. "Well, there were some complications with Caty."

"Caty?" Austin repeats. "What else happened with Caty?"

"She kind of... is trying to threaten me. Us," Jack explains.

"*What?*"

"Yeah."

"What does she want?" Adeel asks.

Jack explains her demands about him leaving Cecil because he's Caty's boyfriend and looks around at the disgusted faces of his teammates.

"She wants *what?*" Lydia stands from her place on the bed and puts her hands on her head. "That's so messed up!"

"What are you gonna do?" Ferris asks.

"If we continue to be public, she said she's gonna get rid of the group."

"We can hide. We don't have to go public," Cecil says but Jack can see the sadness in his eyes.

"No," Jack says. "No, I'm not going to make you do that."

Austin clears his throat. "You know, she didn't even say what she'd do. She's probably bluffing."

Jack nods. Possibly.

"Yeah, I mean, what could she have on us?" Lydia asks. "Our records are squeaky clean, right guys?"

Ferris coughs loudly and the team looks at them. They shrug. "I live a wild life."

"Okay," Austin says. "Well, I say go public and fuck the consequences."

Jack nods again.

"Are y'all sure?" Cecil asks. "Jack, I don't want you to lose your group just because of me."

"No, Caty shouldn't have that much power over me. She doesn't."

"So what does that mean?"

"Well, do you want to... date me? For real?"

"Sweetheart, of course."

"Then let's make it official."

"How are you going to do it?" Adeel asks.

Jack smiles.

"Ready?" Cecil asks.

"Of course." Jack rubs Cecil's back as he hits the button to post their photos on Cecil's account. It's just a simple Instagram post with a picture of them kissing, then a picture of them smiling at the camera.

Cecil looks down at Jack from where he sits in his lap. "We did it."

"We did it." Jack smiles up at him and Cecil leans down to kiss him.

"Ugh!"

"Ew!"

"Get a room!"

"Hey, this *is* our room," Cecil points out.

"Not tonight it's not," Austin says. "Adeel and Ferris are in here. Lydia and Cecil are with me."

"What?"

"We're adults," Jack says.

"Relax, Jack," Lydia says. "Austin's just trying to prevent a pregnancy. Imagine the scandal then!"

Jack doesn't miss Adeel's intensely confused expression.

CHAPTER 19

That night is Jack's best night of sleep in the last week (aside from the night he spent cuddling Cecil). Adeel's snoring and Ferris's disconcerting sleep talk practically rock him to sleep.

Jack can't say the same thing about Cecil, who has dark circles around his eyes and practically falls asleep in his eggs at breakfast.

"Dreams again?" Jack asks him quietly.

Cecil nods his head.

As soon as breakfast is done and they return to the hotel room, Jack gets a call.

"Hello?"

"Hi, Jack. Just wanted to let you know the funeral went well. You were missed," a stern voice says on the other end.

"Sorry, dad. I'm glad it went well."

"Would have been better with your eulogy."

Jack sighs. What is the point of guilting him? It's already over. "Sorry, dad," he repeats.

Cecil looks at him with concern and the rest of the team stops speaking.

"I'm sure you're very busy. I'll let you go," Jack's father says. They say goodbye and the call ends.

Jack sighs heavily and sits on the edge of the bed.

Lydia sits next to him and rubs a reassuring hand on his back. "What's going on, Jackie-poo?"

"Mel's memorial was today."

Austin covers his mouth. "Oh my god, I never would have told you to come back if I'd known."

"No, it's okay. Mel wouldn't want some stuffy funeral anyway. She wanted me to be here."

Cecil smiles at him from the couch.

Jack's heart jumps as he glances at the time. Only 4 more hours until the Amerigo House, simultaneously not enough time to prepare and way too long to wait.

"What's the play for the Amerigo House?" Jack asks.

"Well, it's tricky," Austin says, turning in his chair at the desk. "It's a tourist attraction, you know? Kind of a museum. They rely on the ghost being there. But they're so confident that no one can banish their demon that they actually encourage teams to try. So we're going to treat it like a regular house call, with the end goal of getting rid of the presence."

Jack nods.

"With Cecil around, that demon doesn't stand a chance!" Adeel says.

Cecil laughs and says, "Thank you for the vote of confidence, my friend. This will actually be my first demon."

"Demons aren't real," Jack says out of habit.

Finally, it comes time for the team to leave, and it's the longest thirty-minute car ride of Jack's life. His father's EMF meter sits heavy in his pocket.

After the interminable drive finally ends, Jack looks up and sees the object of years of excitement and intrigue: the Amerigo House. It looks... surprisingly normal. It was built in the mid-80s with blocky architecture and a Spanish tile roof. It's stucco'd and painted a burnt orange.

Austin goes ahead to greet the museum owners and gets the final go-ahead to come in and set up. Adeel gets out his camera and films every step of the process. This has been their most anticipated stop on the tour, so they aren't wasting any opportunities to film, even going as far as strapping GoPros to Lydia and Jack. They're expecting this video alone to get enough views to put them over the top and save the show.

Ferris and Adeel have been editing every episode along the way and posted their most recent stop during the week Jack was gone. It did relievingly well, currently sitting at around two million views. They're hoping this final video garners even more, saving their show once and for all.

"Alright, team. Are we ready?"

"Ready."

They walk to the front door and step into the house. All the lights are off except for the exit signs, casting a red glow across the home.

Jack takes a deep breath. He's finally here. He has wanted to come debunk their demon theories for the longest time, and that day is finally here.

"Oh, goodness," Jack hears from beside him. He turns and Cecil is leaning against the wall, chest heaving.

"Cecil?" Jack grabs his shoulder and Cecil clutches his arm.

"I'm—Oh goodness, this house," he laughs weakly. "I'm okay, I'm okay." A look of pain twists across Cecil's face.

"What is it?" Austin asks.

Cecil grasps the hem of his shirt and slowly lifts it up. Jack shines his flashlight there, revealing three angry, red scratches.

"Cecil..." Lydia says, hand covering her mouth.

Cecil's knees buckle and Jack wraps both arms around him to keep him on his feet.

"Take him to the couch," Austin instructs, and Jack and Adeel walk Cecil to the small sofa and help him sit down.

"What's going on?" Ferris asks.

"The energy in this house, I—" Cecil grabs Jack's arm with one hand and places his other over the scratches on his chest. "Jack, I'm seeing the face. I think it's a demon," he says quietly.

That's impossible. Demons aren't real. Entities can't touch people. Can't scratch people. Can't—Jack places a hand over Cecil's on his chest and breathes heavily.

Psychics are real.

What if demons are too?

Cecil pats his hand. "I'm feeling some better already. Sitting is helping, I think. I can continue the walkthrough soon, just..." He lets his head drop back against the cushions and says, "give me a minute."

Austin shakes his head. "No, not if it's affecting you like this. If it's okay with you, Cecil, I think we'll just have to do this one without you."

"Is that... possible?" Adeel asks.

"We've been checking for ghosts for years, guys. Banishing has been nice, but let's get back to the basics. You know what? It's kind of fitting for our final stop. Back to our roots."

Now that the team has their marching orders, they begin their walkthrough like normal, Ferris with Jack, and Adeel with Lydia.

Jack has his array of devices in his hands and on his belt, and he feels the weight of his father's EMF meter in his back pocket. He takes a breath. He's prepared for this.

Jack and Ferris climb the stairs. He reaches the second floor and begins combing through each room, keeping an eye on his devices. Levels are fluctuating slightly, but nothing that suggests demon infestation like so many believe.

"Anything yet?" Jack asks Ferris, who shakes their head.

"Minor blips but nothing compelling yet."

"Same here."

"It's weird," Ferris says. "With such a major manifestation—the scratches, I mean—you'd think there'd be more on the meters."

This entity is definitely behaving abnormally. Jack wonders if he can trust his gadgets like usual.

They reach the end of the hallway and Jack spots the attic access. He pushes the cover up and to the side and slides the ladder down.

"I'm gonna go up here," he says to Ferris. He hands them the meters he's holding and climbs up before turning around and grabbing them back.

Jack sits back on his heels and shines his flashlight around the space.

For once, he senses the energy himself before his devices detect it.

CHAPTER 20

"Anything?" Ferris calls up to Jack.

"Yeah," Jack replies as his skin crawls. "Hey, I'm gonna film from in here. You go let the others know... I think I found the entity."

Ferris gasps and hurries back down the stairs to the first floor.

Jack slides the cover back over the entrance. The ceiling of the attic is low and beams cross even lower, so Jack crawls on his knees further into the space. He sits down and crosses his legs, placing each of his sensors on the floor in front of him.

Jack's father's words ring in his ears: *There is never a reason to contact an entity.* But as Jack has discovered, not everything is so black and white.

Jack clears his throat. "Hello. My name is Jack." He takes a deep breath and searches for what to say next. "How are you?" Nope. The entity can't talk. Moving on. "Uh... Sorry. I don't really know how to talk to you. I'm really not supposed to talk to entities. I never do. My dad always told me there is never, ever, a single reason to rely on feelings over data. But my aunt died, and I needed to speak to her again, and I discovered... even in a rule that's so hard and fast, there's a gray area." Jack pauses and looks at the meters in front of him. Their readings are astronomical. The entity is right in front of him. "There's a lot of gray area, I guess... You know what?" Jack mutters, and one by one, he picks up each device and turns it off, even his flashlight. He leaves his night vision GoPro on, though, knowing the rage Austin and Ferris would feel if he left them without this footage. He reaches into his pocket and pulls out his father's EMF meter and places it in front of him, and the red bulb is illuminated. The hair on the back of his neck stands up but he swallows his fear like pride.

"Maybe my dad was wrong. Maybe it's okay not to understand things. My boyfriend is on the first floor. It's really new. I only just stopped hating him, since he's a psychic," Jack explains, then realizes those two statements don't connect for anyone but himself. "Well—okay, so, I always hated psychics. I thought they were all frauds. But he was able to contact my aunt. Until then, I thought he was a total fake. My dad told me they all were, so in my world, there was no way they *could* exist. No way talking to an entity would be better than relying on data, but my dad was lying all this time. So here we are."

Jack searches the darkness for another pair of eyes, seeking some kind of human connection with this being who appears to be right in front of him like it's listening. Cecil got scratched. There are other accounts of visitors being pushed, hit, bitten. None of that has happened to Jack, though the entity has had ample opportunity. Maybe it really is listening like it seems to be.

"I'm not afraid of you right now, I don't think. I am a little afraid, but I think it's a more generalized anxiety, actually. This is kind of a new situation for me. It's weird that I can't understand you, yanno? All my life I've tried to understand things to make them less scary. That also sort of means if I can't study something, then it's scary by default. But... I'm not afraid of you."

A wave of grief hits him, but it's not only for Mel. It's for his own life. Jack realizes that if he had taken a few moments to confront his fears instead of feeding into them, his life could have been so much freer. He's only 26 and presumably still has plenty of time ahead of him, but he will never get the joy back that he left on the table. He will never see the sunsets he missed when he focused too hard on the rest of the sky's darkness.

His fear of the unknown stole his life from him. Tears sting his eyes.

"I don't think you're a demon, at least not in that sense. I know that's kind of bold because I really don't know you that well. But I think you're a person whose next life left them behind. I am so sorry your life is over. I am so sorry you feel like you have to stay here. But you don't. There is more after this. Your..." Jack struggles to find the word, "essence. Your essence has moved on, is in another body somewhere. Or a tree, maybe. This life has ended, but you can continue on in that one." Jack takes a breath. "I don't understand how, and there is no way for me to ever understand until I die, but it's true." He shrugs. "It's true enough." *It's true enough.*

Mel is in some other body somewhere. Her essence has started over, has forgotten all about him, has no memory of the years they spent together, of their phone conversations, of the smiles they shared. She doesn't even love him anymore, not in that body.

But her essence still exists, still remembers, still guides him. Jack feels warmth in his chest and reaches his hand up. He never was open enough before, but now he feels her with him. He lets out a breath and closes his eyes.

"Go," he says to the entity. "Go live another life. Your essence will remember this one. It wasn't for nothing."

Jack opens his eyes and sees that the attic is glowing green like the bottom bunk at Mel's; the EMF meter's green light is on. Levels are within normal range. Jack flicks his flashlight back on and moves the attic cover aside. Light floods in and Jack blinks, extending the ladder.

He sees his friends, his team, his family, waiting for him at the bottom. Jack passes his gear to them and climbs down to meet them.

Ferris and Adeel have their cameras trained on him.

"Well?" Lydia asks.

"It's gone." Jack smiles, sadness settled safely into the corners of his mouth. Grief has attached itself to his heart, and Jack knows it's not something that ever goes away. It just nestles deeper and sleeps within him until it's awoken by a familiar perfume, a sunset she would have loved, or a simple passing thought about the strongest woman he has ever known.

She is living, somewhere in the world. He will never meet her again, never hear her voice again, and that's okay. Her essence remembers him, and that's enough.

"Are you okay?" Lydia asks, and Jack realizes tears are falling. He wipes his eyes.

"Yeah. I just realized some things, I guess." He smiles. They walk downstairs and he spots Cecil on the couch. Jack walks over and sits next to him and places a hand on his knee. "How are you doing?"

"Better now," Cecil flirts.

"Really?"

"Actually yes. My lightheadedness is gone, and I think the inflammation around the scratches is going down. Still need to wash them though," Cecil says. Then his eyes go wide and he snaps his head to look at Jack. "Did you—"

Jack smiles.

"Jack, that's amazing!" Cecil exclaims. "What changed? Why were you able to do it?"

"I guess you rubbed off on me."

Cecil smiles. "You know, I *could* teach you to tune into your psychic abilities if you want."

"Oh, god no. I just started accepting all this. Don't push it."

"I'll get you one day. Maybe I'll take you to see a psychic reader in California."

"California?" Lydia repeats.

"Yeah. We're gonna visit soon," Cecil says, lacing his fingers with Jack's.

"I'm *not* having my fortune read."

"We'll see if it's... *in the cards.*"

Jack laughs and rolls his eyes at the pun. "Come on. Someone has to tell the owners they don't have a tourist attraction anymore."

CHAPTER 21

The next morning finds the team still riding the high of finishing their tour on such a good note. Cecil and Jack sit side by side on one of the beds, Jack's arm around him.

"Hello," Cecil says, looking up at him.

"Hi." Jack kisses him on the nose. Cecil catches him before he pulls away and gives him a slow, lingering kiss.

"Hey lovebirds," Lydia says as she throws a pillow at them. "Knock it off! Some of us are still painfully single."

"That's not what you want the internet to think," Cecil quips.

"When are we leaving?" Adeel asks Austin, who is lounging on the other bed.

"Checkout is at 11 and I don't feel like driving yet, so 11."

"I can drive," Cecil offers.

"No, he can't," Jack says, "if you want to get home within the next year. He drives five miles an hour."

"I do not!"

"You do, I looked at the speedometer. Five."

Cecil tries to shrug his arm off, but Jack wraps the other around him, trapping him. Cecil laughs.

"Alright. The last video has been up for about ten hours now," Austin says. The team had stayed up late last night editing. "We're currently at..." Austin pauses for suspense, then says, "eight million views." The team gasps. "Apparently we went viral on Twitter. Camilla tweeted about it."

"So is that enough to save the show?" Cecil asks.

"We'll know for sure soon. I should be getting a call from Funbuzz shortly."

Jack takes a deep breath. If nothing ever changes again, that'd be okay with him. He wishes he could remain on tour with his favorite people forever.

Jack closes his eyes and savors the sound of Adeel and Lydia bickering, of the birds outside the window, of the light drone of the hotel air conditioner, of a phone ringing—

Jack's eyes snap open and he meets the alarmed eyes of his teammates. They all look to Austin who holds his empty hands up. Then Jack sees that it's Cecil's phone ringing.

"Sorry guys, one sec." Cecil steps out into the hallway.

A few moments later, Austin's phone rings for real, and he answers it, the whole team waiting with bated breath.

"Hello? Yes... Uh-huh." There is a very long pause before Austin says, "Absolutely, no I understand...Yes...Okay, Tuesday, you said..? Okay, talk then. Bye."

Austin lowers his phone and takes a deep breath. He looks around at each of them before shaking his head.

"Come on man, that's not funny," Ferris says, desperation in their voice.

"Not joking. Funbuzz is not renewing us for another season," Austin says with a heavy sigh.

Jack's stomach falls. This can't be real.

"Wait, but why?" Ferris asks. "We've been getting millions of views."

Austin nods. "Lydia, Adeel," he begins, "unfortunately, someone complained to corporate. They said the unbalanced power dynamic of your 'relationship' made them uncomfortable and fear for Adeel's safety."

"Well at least someone noticed," Adeel says, trying to see the bright side, but Lydia shakes her head.

"Not the time, man."

Cecil walks back into the room and looks around at the team's faces, immediately sensing the energy change. "What's... going on?"

"We got canceled," Ferris informs him.

Cecil covers his mouth. "What? But y'all worked so hard."

"Adeel and Lydia worked harder," Ferris says.

Lydia covers her face with her hands and Adeel wipes his eyes.

"Who was on your phone call, Cecil?" Austin asks.

"Hm? Oh, it was just the airline." Cecil glances at Jack.

The team continues chatting dejectedly.

Jack's phone buzzes.

Unknown

Sorry Jackie

I know no one likes a tattletale :)

He doesn't reply, and just slips his phone back in his pocket. Figures she'd be the one to take them down. One last squeeze of his ass. But Jack feels like he won anyway. He gets Cecil.

Jack walks over to Cecil and quietly says, "Walk outside with me."

The pair walks into the hallway and Jack puts his hands on Cecil's shoulders.

Cecil stalls. "I'm sorry about your show, Jack, but now you can start Finch Paranormal—"

"Cec, that wasn't the airline. Be honest with me."

Cecil looks at him, concerned. "I don't know..."

"Go on."

Cecil takes a breath. "It was my agent. She said that this tour has really improved my reputation online and... several publishers are interested in my book deal."

Jack laughs excitedly. "Cecil, that's great!" Jack pulls him into a tight hug. When he pulls back, he sees Cecil's eyes filled with tears. "Why aren't you excited?"

"Because your show just got canceled, and here I am with good news."

Jack searches his eyes. It's more than that. Jack gives him a look. "What else?"

"It just doesn't feel like a good time to tell you."

"Tell me anyway."

"I got picked up for a very small, not-a-big-deal... Netflix mini-series."

Jack's eyes go wide and he hugs him again. "Cecil, that's everything you wanted!"

Cecil adds, "It's super small, only 8 episodes."

Jack hugs him tighter and Cecil laughs. Jack says, "8 episodes? That's amazing! Cecil, I am so proud of you. You deserve it. When does filming start?"

"Next month."

Jack's smile fades. "But that means..."

"Yeah."

Jack nods. He knew their California trip was too good to be true.

Cecil squeezes Jack's hands. "One day, I swear."

"Okay, that's okay. We can do long distance. We can FaceTime every night, and take turns flying out, and—"

Cecil smiles sadly. "Jack, we're both so busy. I have my show, you'll have your business, right?"

Jack nods.

"Do you really think it can work right now?"

"I—" Jack sighs and shakes his head. No, he doesn't. But Cecil is everything Jack has ever wanted, and they found each other out of eight billion people in the world, in all this mess. He sacrificed their show to be together, and after everything, it's just not the right time? Jack swallows. They haven't even had a chance to fall in love.

Jack lets out a breath and pulls Cecil into another hug. He cups Cecil's face and kisses him, a goodbye to what might have been if things were different. Jack wonders if Mel is seeing this. He hopes she's proud of how hard he fought for him.

"So do you know what you want to write your book about?"

Cecil smiles. "I have an idea."

Jack and Cecil walk back into the hotel room. Jack takes a deep breath and looks around. This is probably the last time all these people will be in the same room at the same time.

He can see the sun through the sheer curtains, and he smiles. These people are resilient. They'll be okay. Jack will be okay too. He learned there is more to the world than he can understand, more than he can experience himself, and for once that doesn't scare him.

Jack Finch, the skeptical ghost hunter. Maybe not such a skeptic anymore.

CHAPTER 22

12 MONTHS LATER

Jack unlocks the door to his office. He thinks of it as his office, anyway. It's really more of a storefront in a mostly vacant strip mall. He glances at the sign leaning against the wall. He still needs to put that up, so he adds it to his mental to-do list but will certainly forget about it again in a matter of hours. Jack tilts his head to read it and smiles even though he's read it countless times since it arrived: *Finch Paranormal, LLC.*

Jack sets his messenger bag down in the chair at his desk and walks to the back of the office. He opens the cabinet and pulls out his case of gear, then sits it down on the desk, a puff of dust dissipating in the air. Work has been a little... slow as he gets started. But that doesn't mean he's not proud of what he does.

Jack does house calls now, not for cameras, not for audiences, but for himself, the homeowner, and the entity. His father would never say it, but Jack would like to think he's making him proud by not turning specters into spectacles.

Jack's phone buzzes and he's reminded that not everyone lives by those words.

Austin

Hey buddy, we're at the motel

The other Ghost Checkers continued making videos after their show was canceled. They bought the rights to the name and made their own channel, and lucky for them, a lot of their viewership migrated with them.

They started partnering with famous YouTubers and doing collab after collab. It seems to work for them. They were recently invited to a big YouTube convention and held a meet and greet that went a lot better than the one in Virginia. Lydia had sent him selfies with a long line of fans waiting to meet them. Jack smiles as he thinks about it, hundreds of smiling faces excited to meet them. He's glad they've found the success they deserve.

Jack

See you soon

After confirming that all the necessary gear is in the case, Jack flips the lid and latches it closed, the draft sending a few papers flying off his desk. He bends to pick them back up and smiles when he grabs a purple note with glittery ink on it.

He had received this note a month or so ago when Cecil sent him an advance copy of his book: *Then, Now, and Soon: How the Passed Can Change Our Future*. The note had no words, just a poorly drawn ghost and a heart.

Jack glances at the book where it sits on his shelf. When he first received it, he flipped through it quickly, appreciating the fact Cecil thought to send him a copy, but no part of him felt like sitting down to read some ghost-written celebrity memoir. Then he noticed a dog-eared page.

The marked chapter was entitled "My Time with the Ghost Checkers". Jack quickly realized they were all mentioned by name as Cecil recounted their time together, every Lydia and Ferris antic, every adorable Adeel moment. Cecil ended the chapter by saying, *Passed loved ones aren't the only ones who can teach us about the beyond. Sometimes it just takes a change of perspective. Just ask Jack.*

Jack smiles and his heart jumps as he remembers where he's about to go.

He grabs the case and his bag and heads toward the door but stops and returns to the cabinet. His eyes scan the contents until he spots it: his dad's EMF meter. He pockets it and returns to the door, locking it behind himself and heading to his car.

It's a long drive to the Honey Motel, their meeting place. Austin had texted him a few weeks ago and asked if he'd be free. Jack fought his excitement and waited a minute or two before answering. (Lydia taught him to do that so he wouldn't seem so desperate over text.) His answer was 'yes,' of course.

Finally, he pulls up to the salmon-pink motel. Each room has an air conditioner hanging out of the window, and in the center of the complex, there is a dingy pool right next to a dumpster. It reminds him of the motels he and Austin would stay at during the early days of The Ghost Checkers when their budget was in the negatives and all they had was each other.

Jack steps out of the car and takes a deep breath. It smells like early adulthood and big dreams.

He scrolls up in his conversation with Austin and finds the room number: 214. Jack hoists his suitcase out of his trunk, shrugs on his messenger bag, and grabs his gear case before climbing the stairs to the second floor of rooms.

Adrenaline sparks low in his stomach as he knocks on the door. He takes a moment to straighten his shirt and smooth his hair. There is a commotion from inside the room before the door slams open revealing Lydia and Ferris, each fighting to be the first out.

"Jack!" Lydia exclaims as she pushes past Ferris and wraps her arms around Jack.

Jack is knocked backwards by the force of her affection. He wraps an arm around her and smiles when Ferris gets too impatient and joins their hug.

"Jack's here," Adeel says from inside the room, then appears in the doorway. "Hi Jack!"

"Hey buddy!" Jack says. Lydia and Ferris untangle themselves and step back, giving Adeel a turn.

"Come in, come in," Ferris says as they lead Jack into the room.

Jack glances around eagerly, but his vision gets filled with a smiling face.

"Jackie!" Austin says, all his teeth showing in the kind of smile that can't be faked. He clutches Jack's shoulders, then pulls him in for a hug. "I've missed you so much, buddy."

Then Jack sees him.

"Jack, we have so much to tell you!" Ferris says, tugging on Jack's arm. "Okay, so last week—"

"No, don't tell him that yet, you have to tell him about Padma," Lydia butts in.

"Guys," Austin says.

"Let me tell the story—"

"You're telling it wrong—"

"Guys!" Austin says again. Ferris and Lydia stop bickering. "Let's maybe go outside, yeah?" Austin winks and shepherds the others out of the room.

Jack returns his attention to the bed.

Cecil stands up, wringing his hands.

He looks just how Jack expected, golden hair falling in curls around his face, a little longer than when he last saw him.

His freckles are darker, or maybe there are more, and they dust his nose perfectly like they were placed there by the gods themselves.

Jack drops his bags and walks towards him. He takes a deep breath.

"Hello," Cecil says. His smile is more confident, and his eyes swim with a hopefulness that makes Jack's heart ache.

"Hi."

ABOUT THE AUTHOR

Connor Bryan began writing stories in 2nd grade with a crayon-illustrated series entitled *Cat and Mouse*. Her passion for writing never left her and developed into a love of poetry and fiction. She writes and lives in central Florida. To learn more about Connor and her writing, visit connorbryanwrites.com or follow @conbryanwrites on Instagram and Twitter.